Books by Richard S. Platz

PROJECT DIVINE WIND

APPOINTMENT AT ANGAHUAN
(Co-Authored with James A. Kline)

OF MAGIC AND DELUSION
A Tale Whispered to the Author by the One True God

by Richard S. Platz

Blue Lake Press

Cover Design by Annie Reid

BLUE LAKE PRESS
A Western Division Subsidiary of the
Chicago, Whitewater & Mad River Company
P O Box 797, Blue Lake, CA 95525

ISBN: 978-0615527086

OF MAGIC AND DELUSION

A Tale Whispered to the Author by the One True God

Dedicated to the Memory of

**Moses, Jesus, Mohammad,
Joseph Smith, and L. Ron Hubbard,**

All Dead,

And to all who have heard the whisper

Of magic and delusion

CHAPTER ONE

The Appearance of Conflict

Surrender!" bellowed the mammoth warrior, looming like an unclean gorilla beside his dwarfed, grizzled, and idiotically grinning companion. Bound in motley rags caked with dried blood and filth, the giant scratched and swaggered, an offense to the polished marble of the great throne room. He spat through the cloud of flies surrounding him, and the yellowish spittle caught and ran down a sculptured marble column.

The King of Nod gripped with a fierce determination the exquisitely carved armrests of his throne, his white knuckles concealed by the elegant silk vestments. His jaw was set, his muscles tense, his heart pounding fiercely, but he was unsure of what to do or say. He prayed for inspiration in dealing with this brutal messenger from the barbarian army claiming ancestral rights to his kingdom. The King was still reeling from two staggering blows fate had recently delivered. Two years ago his young queen had quietly bled to death in childbirth, and last year his father had fallen in battle, allowing the regency to devolve untimely upon his unprepared shoulders. Now Barth strutted before him like an angel of doom come to administer a third and fatal coup de grace.

"Lay down your arms and disband your army, or by the vengeance of Allah the Exactor, we'll crush your kingdom, slaughter your puny soldiers, and rape your whoring wives." In an involuntary obeisance to his deity, Barth's powerful hand grasped the hilt of his great broadsword.

Longbow men on each side of the King raised their bows, pointing twenty razor-tipped arrows at the behemoth's hairy chest.

Barth laughed at them and spat again, for he was the mightiest warrior in the vast and invincible army of the southern wilderness. Had he not been personally appointed by Jabal the Chosen, his mighty warlord, to cross the Great River into Nod and demand absolute capitulation and return of the rich lands which had been stolen from their ancestors.

The King wished his father were still alive. The Old King would no doubt have done something appropriate, something decisive and worthy of honor and respect. For an instant he felt his father's eyes on him, but when he glanced to the side, it was only Grimm, the wily Chief Advisor who had served the Old King so well, watching him, waiting. Grimm, like his father, like everyone in the throne room, expected something from him, and he feared he was about to disappoint them all.

Suddenly an infant, bare-bottomed, beaming, and bloused in gold lamé with "Kingdom of Nod" embroidered across the back, emerged with surprising agility through the line of bowmen and toddled toward the huge warrior. Plopping down at his feet, the infant gaped up at the hulking monster.

"And murder your children!" boomed Barth, drawing his sword and hoisting it overhead, poised to slice the child in two.

"*Hold fast!*" cried the King, springing to his feet. "That is the Crown Prince of Nod! Sheath your blade or you won't live to carry our reply back to Jabal!" The tips of twenty arrows trembled with the tension of taut bowstrings.

The giant slowly lowered his sword. "And what *is* your reply?"

A terrified wet nurse broke through the phalanx of bowmen, scooped up the bewildered infant, and scurried away to safety.

"We will need time to consider," the King replied, seating himself with a deliberate show of regal ceremony. "What are the terms of our surrender?"

In the shadows of the far corner of the throne room a cloaked figure made some final adjustments to a harness buckled about his waist, closed his robes, fiddled with a small canister in his left hand, and nodded to another figure concealed behind the columns on the opposite side of the large chamber.

Barth spat again. "We demand *total* surrender, and you'll learn the terms as we tell 'em to you." He roared at his own cleverness and, looking down, slapped his absently grinning companion on the back of the head. Then he turned back to the King. "You have two weeks, and not a day more. By then our boats will be finished, and our warriors ready to cross the Great River. In two weeks we'll enter your cowardly kingdom, with your permission or without it." Barth slipped the gleaming broadsword back into his scabbardless belt and turned to leave.

"Wait!" the King called out, searching for a way to stall the messenger a little longer.

Barth stopped and looked back over his shoulder.

"We will have an answer for you before that time," the King pronounced slowly. In the shadows behind Barth a movement caught his eye. He looked over at Grimm, who nodded silently. The King straightened himself on the throne and cleared his throat like a nervous schoolboy about to recite a difficult lesson. "It is my duty to warn you that you may leave us no choice–"

"No choice but what?" spat Barth, wheeling to face the throne.

"– but to destroy your army," the King continued evenly. "And that of your evil allies across the mountains to the southeast."

"Don't mock me!" snarled the monster, his huge hand again grasping the hilt of his broadsword, "or by the Dogs of the Dead you'll not live the two weeks to be dethroned!"

A flame was ignited in the dimness behind Barth. Overhead wires twanged softly.

"By what power would you resist our forces?" the giant challenged.

"By the power of the Sorcerer of Nod," replied the King.

"Who?"

Brilliant flares flashed afire behind the huge warrior, and as he spun around in confusion, out of the flames the cloaked figure arose as gracefully as a bird and flew slowly toward him. Barth fell to one knee and raised his arm to shield his eyes from the blinding light.

"By *my* powers," thundered the voice of the flying figure, reverberating eerily from two acoustic dishes which had snapped open above him like the shells of an agitated clam. "And by the powers of sorcery. Take back this message: send your troops home from our borders and leave us in peace, or suffer a horrible scourge before a single soldier has set foot upon the soil of Nod." The Sorcerer pointed his finger at Barth, and instantly a fireball shot forth from his hand and caromed off the giant's ragged chest. The Sorcerer banked gracefully into a cloud of smoke and was gone.

Barth staggered to his feet, bewildered and unsteady, and dragging his cringing comrade by the scruff of the neck, fled the throne room beating distractedly at his smoldering robes. The chamber doors thundered closed behind them.

The King clung to the arms of the throne, drawing measured breaths, until his trembling had subsided. When he had regained some composure, he arose and clapped his hands. "Bravo, Sorcerer, very convincing. But how did you do that?"

From behind the tall velvet drapes covering the wall to the King's left, the Sorcerer emerged. The hood of his cloak was thrown back, revealing a handsome, youthful face, incongruously framed by prematurely silvering hair and beard. He coiled a long wire as he approached the throne. "A Sorcerer never reveals his secrets," he replied, "even to kings."

"Well done, nonetheless. Well done, indeed." The King was beaming now. He turned to Grimm, who was never far from his side. "Don't you agree?"

The Chief Advisor was a stocky, bushy-eyebrowed bear of a man. The Old King had placed absolute confidence in him for more than forty years. Grimm wore his perennial scowl like an approaching thunderstorm wears dark shadows. "I think you should see that Barth and his sniveling companion are afforded safe conduct to the border and back across the Great River. He should not be detained whatever outrage he may commit on his journey back." Grimm's eyes narrowed to slits of lightning flashing beneath his cumulus eyebrows. "It is important that Barth returns with his report to Jabal the Chosen."

"Yes, of course." The King grasped the lapel of an attendant stationed beside the throne and pulled him close. "You heard the Chief Advisor?"

"Yes, your highness."

"Well, see that it's done."

The attendant bowed and rushed out through a passageway

concealed by the tapestry behind the throne.

"It appeared for a moment our plans would be undone," the King remarked, "when the Prince blundered out to confront our unwelcome visitors."

"You handled it quite well, my lord," the Sorcerer responded, and all the attendants and archers murmured assent.

"Do you really think so?" The King was pleased with himself.

"It was fortunate your bowmen restrained themselves," Grimm rumbled. "I think it's time to clear the court, your highness. Ask the Sorcerer to remain."

While the attendants and soldiers were departing, the King asked his Chief Advisor in a lowered voice, "Do you really think this . . . display . . . will do any good?" His brow was deeply furrowed. "Will it forestall the attack?"

"Barth was impressed, my lord. But I would be very surprised if Jabal gives his story much credence. We can only hope that word of Barth's obvious fright will spread through the ranks and weaken the fighting resolve of his comrades at arms."

"Yes," the King sighed. He shook his head ruefully. "But even so, our small army will be no match for countless hordes of fanatics bent on recovering what they believe we stole from them." The King looked small and frightened. "I wonder what father would have done?"

When the door had closed behind the last attendant, Grimm turned angrily to the Sorcerer. "Why in God's name did you add that business about the terrible scourge? Now they'll find out in time it was all an empty bluff."

The Sorcerer ignored the Chief Advisor and knelt before the King. The clear fire in his eyes was eclipsed for an instant by a memory of personal tragedy. He shuddered, then spoke in a frighteningly quiet voice, "My liege, my threat to Barth was not empty. The power of sorcery shall prevail. It's inexorable course has already begun." A tear rolled inexplicably down his cheek. "Your enemies will be destroyed. Your kingdom spared."

The King clutched the Sorcerer's sleeve. "If you can do this, you may choose your own reward. That is my solemn pledge."

The claim of Jabal the Chosen and his followers to all the lands of Nod was not entirely without basis. It was indeed Jabal's ancestor, and not the King's, who had first wandered into the great valley and claimed it for his descendants, founding the ancient city of Enoch, which he named after his firstborn. But Jabal's ancestors were nomads and wanderers, living in tents, following their herds wherever the untilled land would sustain them, and Nod had yielded its fruits to them only grudgingly. Like vagabonds they drifted from place to place, across the Great River and beyond, forever homeless.

It was ancestors of the King who had later migrated into the territory, settling it, civilizing it, digging irrigation channels and dams, building villages and towns and cities, constructing roads, reclaiming fertile cropland from the parched desert and impenetrable chaparral of the rolling foothills. Farm by farm, field by field, fence by fence, the King's ancestors had slowly tamed the land, assimilating a few of Jabal's people, and displacing the rest.

As the population multiplied with the passing years, the inhabitants of Nod managed to eke out a modest existence for themselves by careful planning, husbandry, and small but reliable harvests from their farms and ranches. The natural grazing lands upon which the nomads depended, however, could not keep pace with expanded use, and in lean years, Jabal's forebears fought with one another for what little there was. The cost of defeat was often starvation. Conflict spawned a class of nomad warriors, marauding bands of soldiers under the command of a petty warlord, stealing what they needed, preying upon the weak, and skilled swordsmen and archers retained by the powerful tribal chiefs to increase their wealth and defend what they had taken from others.

To protect its subjects, the Kingdom of Nod established a small but efficient militia. It was all that was needed. The Great River to the south and the ragged Eastern Range of mountains, whose summits and ridges defined the boundary to the east, provided natural barriers to the ravaging barbarians. Only an occasional party of adventuresome marauders ever managed to cross into Nod to steal the fruits of the more gentle society, and such incursions were easily controlled by the well-trained army of Nod.

Or so things had stood before the vision of Jabal the Chosen. Jabal was a fierce young warrior of great skill and cunning who professed one day that an angel of Allah had appeared to him in a dream and appointed him to unite all the warring tribes under his exclusive command for the holy purpose of retaking the lands of Nod, which rightfully belonged to his people. He had been chosen by God as their savior and deliverer. Through a series of treaties, intrigues, betrayals, deceptions, and bloody battles, Jabal the Chosen won over or overpowered nearly all the tribal chieftains and warlords. He mercilessly slaughtered the remaining opposition and consolidated his command over all the nomad troops south of the Great River. Terror and promise of reward sustained his tenuous alliance, while he pandered his divine mission to the superstitious and gullible, who turned out to include most of his troops. His warriors numbered in the tens of thousands, and though undisciplined, they made up in religious zeal for what they lacked in military finesse. They outnumbered the defenders of Nod by fifty to one.

The Old King had sent a select group of special envoys to Jabal in the hope of negotiating a peaceful settlement of their territorial dispute and averting war. These were fine counselors, reasonable men learned in property rights, surveying, land titles, adverse possession, and eminent domain. Jabal the Chosen laughed and lopped off their heads. His command found its legitimacy in his divinely inspired mission of overthrowing the Kingdom of Nod by force of arms, and any deviation from that course might undermine the alliance itself. Compromise was out of the question.

Six weeks later the Old King fell in glorious hand-to-hand battle with Jabal himself. Or so the story was told. Actually he cut his heel on the rusty sword of a fallen comrade and contracted lockjaw. As his father before him, the Old King jealously preserved his direct command over the troops, and while personally leading a force of crack horsemen against a bandit gang which had been terrorizing the villages along the southern border, he had fallen into a trap set by Jabal the Chosen. Beneath the blackness of a new moon, the Old King had led a bold escape, but he had sustained the seemingly minor injury in the process. He was dead before the moon again was full.

Grimm had borne the tragic news to his new lord and master. Just after breakfast the King was on his way out to the fields for a rousing croquet match with his cronies who had all grown middle-aged waiting for that day.

"Your father has fallen in battle," Grimm had told him. "You are now the King and must take charge. It is up to you to settle matters with Jabal the Chosen."

The Old King had always appeared larger than life to his son. Each footstep he was to follow in seemed so big it would swallow him completely and leave no trace. The forty-year-old regent listened speechlessly to his Chief Advisor. Then he fainted.

The subjects of Nod were not warlike by nature. As news of the impending invasion spread, panic increased and threatened to overthrow the new King's tenuous reign even before he could be deposed by the invading hordes. Wealthy landowners hastily gathered together whatever valuables they could and scurried frantically around in circles. The kingdom was an island of culture within a sea of mindless barbarism. There was no place to go. Peasants abandoned their ripening fields, preferring to spend their last few days at home with family. Everywhere merchants, shopkeepers, and tradesmen stopped work and, gazing toward the southern horizon, sniffed the breeze and wondered what the hell the King planned to do about Jabal.

The day after Barth left the castle and the Sorcerer had returned in haste to his home atop one of the tall peaks in the Eastern Range, Grimm sat the King down and tried to discuss military strategy with him. Jabal had managed to enlist the savage mountain tribes of the east into his alliance and was planning a pincer attack on the kingdom from the south and east. Troops stood poised at the borders of Nod to begin his self-proclaimed holy vendetta. A line of defense had to be established.

But the King wanted nothing to do with it. He shuddered to choose between losing a savage war and the doom of unconditional surrender. In terror and confusion he proclaimed Grimm to be Commander-in-Chief of all the armed forces of Nod and fled to his private chamber to await the outcome. He had been curiously heartened by the wizard's terse assurances, though he carefully avoided inquiry into the man's methods and means. Silently he cheered him on.

CHAPTER TWO

An Accommodation Is Reached

General Grimm did not share the King's naive optimism. To kill a serpent, one must crush its head. Victory would have to be fought for and won. Though he had barely a thousand men in his command, he devised a plan. He would divide his troops into two battalions. One would spread out along the banks of the Great River to attack the invaders where they were most vulnerable, perhaps sinking a few boats with catapults and huge rocks, at least inflicting casualties on the exposed flotilla with arrows shot from cover. When the enemy had established its beachhead, the battalion would fall back in headlong retreat, hopefully drawing the invaders after them in hot pursuit. The second battalion would conceal itself in the caves of Routh beneath the rough cliffs near the river rapids where the enemy was unlikely to attack. After the first wave of invaders had swept past them, they would emerge and search for the enemy command post. If they were lucky enough to find Jabal the Chosen and kill him, they might have a chance, if not of victory, at least of stalemate. The plan's chances of success were meager, but something had to be tried.

Too quickly the days slipped past. The futility of the situation began to flutter home to roost among Grimm's hapless soldiers, and desertion became popular. Nod's forces dwindled. Riding south to battle against the tide of fleeing refugees, the army of Nod seemed to dissolve into the countryside like sugar into hot coffee. General Grimm arrived at the Great River one morning leading a column of barely a hundred men, those too feebleminded to appreciate a lost cause when it perched on their noses and looked them in the eye.

As the time for the invasion drew near, word came that pockets of illness had begun to break out within the crowded encampments of the barbarians across the Great River. At first the reports attributed the infestation to unsanitary conditions in the camps. A curious pattern of epidemic developed, from west to east along the front. Then the same sickness also struck the mountain tribes at their bivouac on the other side of the monastery pass. Word came that the campaign had been postponed a week to allow the invasion forces time to recover full strength.

The disease was diagnosed as smallpox. Over half its victims were gravely ill, many dying, and the plague was spreading among them like fire through a tinder-dry forest. No one, on either side of the border, doubted any longer that the Sorcerer was the instrument of this terrible scourge.

Jabal the Chosen took sick and retired to his tent. The faithful took it as a sign. Jabal himself would show them how to fight and conquer the devastating disease. The Sorcerer's spell would be broken. They called upon Allah's protection while the invasion force bided its time. When word finally leaked out that Jabal had succumbed, soldiers who had not yet contracted the disease broke ranks and disappeared into the night. The remaining positions were decimated, manned only by dying warriors and those too sick to flee. The battle was over before it had begun, and not a single enemy soldier had set foot within the Kingdom of Nod. Precisely as the Sorcerer had foretold.

When there was no longer any doubt that the Kingdom had been miraculously spared, the King relieved Grimm of his temporary command. His first official act as royal commander was to dishonorably discharge all those who had deserted. They would not be replaced. The kingdom would no longer be burdened with the extravagance of maintaining a standing army, except, of course, for ceremonial functions in and about the castle. With the Sorcerer on their side, who needed one?

The King proclaimed a week-long holiday. Festivities were to culminate in a lush banquet honoring the Sorcerer and investing him with the newly-ordained title of Protector of the Kingdom. Invitations to the feast were inscribed and sent out, and a special envoy was dispatched upon the arduous three-day journey to the wizard's secluded mountaintop retreat to specially request his presence and that of his lovely young wife. The King planned to meet them on the day of the banquet and lead a parade through the main streets of the capital and on to the castle.

In matters of public ceremony and courtly etiquette, the King was without equal. The parade, the banquet, the ceremony of investiture were all planned to the most minute detail. So when the King's minister plenipotentiary returned a day early with the news that the Sorcerer would be unable to participate in the royal proceedings honoring him, the regent was understandably distressed.

"How in the devil's name can we have a banquet in his honor if he refuses to submit?" the King fumed. "How will it look to our subjects if we cannot bring such a powerful man to the castle to honor him? What excuse did he give?"

The ashen minister was obviously unnerved to be the bearer of such bad tidings. Droplets of perspiration beaded on his forehead. He cleared his throat. "He said that there had been a death in the family, your majesty, and that he was therefore indisposed–"

"Indisposed! My God! To an invitation from his King!" The King's mood verged on hysteria.

Grimm, who had resumed his position as Chief Advisor, stepped forward from the darkness behind the messenger. "I instructed you to bring him here by force, if necessary. Why didn't you seize him? Were your orders not clear?"

The messenger spun around and bowed to the stocky advisor. Drops of sweat splattered on the cold marble floor. "We tried, my lord. I had him surrounded by four of the King's best soldiers. When I insisted that he accompany us, he refused. I informed him of my instructions to bring him in fetters if necessary, and he just laughed. On my signal the soldiers leapt to take him captive. Before they could reach him, there was a flash of light and a thick cloud of smoke and flames where he had been standing. It rose up into the trees above us. When the air had cleared, he was gone. There wasn't any trace of him. His house was empty, his wife and attendants gone. We waited half the day, but he never returned."

"How many witnessed this," Grimm asked.

"Only the four soldiers and I, my lord. The rest of our party was camped below the crest and saw and heard nothing."

"Good. And these four soldiers, can they be trusted?"

"Yes, my lord. They are four of the best."

"See that each is promoted and given an increase in pay. Make sure they understand that they're to speak of this to no one."

"It's already been done, my lord."

"Did the Sorcerer say anything else?" Grimm's voice was a low rumble.

"Yes. He gave me a message for the King."

The King eyed his minister suspiciously, as a mouse might eye an envoy from the cat. "What was the message?"

The Minister was miserably uncomfortable. "He said, and I quote," he cleared his throat again, "'If the King wants to see me, tell him to come here.'"

"My God!" The King grabbed his crown to keep it from falling off his head. "How is this going to *look*!"

"Anything else?" Grimm asked.

"That was all, my lord."

Grimm dismissed the minister, and the ebullient envoy fairly danced out of the chamber relishing the heavy bounce of his head still attached to his neck.

"What have we created, Grimm?" the King wanted to know when the throne room was empty. "How does it look if the Sorcerer can resist with impunity the will of the ruler of the kingdom?"

Grimm sat down heavily in the chair just below the King. "I don't think he has any ambitions against the throne, your highness. No, I believe he just wants to be left alone right now. He seems to be possessed of that peculiar sort of overbearing conscience that grieves for the hideous deaths inflicted on our enemies, even as he rejoices with us in the preservation of the kingdom. But he's no threat to you."

"Perhaps not. But how are we going to get out of this embarrassing mess he seems to have placed us in?"

"You could graciously accept his invitation."

"I could?" The notion startled the King into the singular.

"A magnanimous gesture, no doubt."

"Perhaps we could . . . ."

"The King himself, by his own initiative, condescends to pay honor to a great countryman who is unfortunately . . . unable . . . incapable, for whatever reason, of accepting an invitation to the castle."

"Yes, I like it," chortled the King. "We will need to get the wording just right, of course."

"Of course," Grimm rumbled, smiling imperceptibly and scratching out a few notes to himself.

"It's fine weather for a royal outing," the King proclaimed. "And the Prince is now old enough to undertake his first extended journey. It's time he got to know the realm, and the realm got to know him, wouldn't you say?"

"I think it's time you had a talk with your Protector of the Kingdom," Grimm reminded him ominously.

"Yes. I see what you mean. It's time we reached a clear understanding with the Sorcerer. Absolutely. No doubt about it."

The parade and banquet were held as scheduled, but without benefit of the Sorcerer's presence. The official announcement explained in great detail how the wizard had not yet fully recovered from the enormous expenditure of energy involved in single- handedly routing two separate armies. The King himself would travel to the Sorcerer's mountain retreat to personally bestow the supreme honor of Protector of the Kingdom upon the exhausted magician. The two empty chairs beside the King at the head of the banquet table were heralded as ceremonial reminders to the celebrants of the debt the kingdom owed to the Sorcerer and his beautiful wife, but to those few who dared to believe they could see beyond mere appearance, they were tokens of where real domestic power now rested.

And so it came to pass that the King and his elaborate entourage undertook the long journey to the Sorcerer's mountain retreat. The road from the capital city ran generally north-by-northeast and usually took three days to transit. The King's party took six, seeing the sights, visiting an influential farmer here, a rich manufacturer there, entertaining petty functionaries everywhere, and generally dispensing its favors across the countryside. Town streets and village byways were invariably lined with peasants and shopkeepers, merchants and mayors, farmers and homemakers, each hoping to catch a glimpse of the King and his beloved infant son the Prince. Words of praise abounded for the King and the Sorcerer. As royal bugles blared, the subjects cheered wildly to be part of such a wonderful, peaceful, and inviolable kingdom.

The King took the precaution of sending an envoy on ahead to make quite certain the magician intended to receive him in the fashion appropriate to a monarch's visit. The Sorcerer welcomed the honor, it was reported, and would be on his best behavior, though he would prefer that the King limit to ten the number in the royal party that actually made their way up the mountainside to visit the wizard's modest household. This suited the King just fine. Not knowing for certain what pranks the unruly magician might be capable of perpetrating, he was pleased to keep the number of witnesses to an absolute minimum.

But the King need not have worried, for the visit contained not a single awesome act, no pyrotechnics whatsoever, and nothing particularly out of the ordinary. As the King, his Chief Advisor, and the Sorcerer held their private discussions seated informally around the kitchen table, the wizard bounced the infant Prince on his knee. He was truly fond of the inquisitive lad. The youngster was fascinated by the painting of the Sorcerer's strikingly beautiful wife which hung on the wall above the sideboard.

"I'm sorry your wife is unable to receive us," the King said more than once.

"Yes, I'm sorry too," the magician replied each time without attempting to explain her absence.

Grimm diverted the flow of the conversation back into the channel of the business at hand.

"You needn't concern yourselves with my loyalty to you and to the young Prince here," the Sorcerer said, still bouncing the burbling Prince. "I frankly don't care to participate in the customary ceremony of court, splendid though I'm sure it must be. Nevertheless, you will have my continuing allegiance and support in preserving peace in the kingdom and assuring the rule of justice."

"The King will always seek to have his rule tempered with justice," Grimm rumbled.

"Then the King shall have my unswerving allegiance and support."

As Grimm had advised, the King offered the magician a yearly stipend, modest compared to many of the extravagances of the royal court, but fully adequate to meet his needs and those of his staff and household. In exchange, the Sorcerer accepted the title of Protector of the Kingdom as a royal office, implying under the circumstances a continuing duty as well as recognition in thanks for a past task well done. The wizard declined, however, to name any further favor in discharge of the King's earlier pledge of reward, made hastily in the teeth of certain disaster.

Grimm brought up the delicate subject of separation of powers within the kingdom. In a lengthy, though at times oblique discussion which the King had difficulty following, Grimm and the Sorcerer readily agreed that the magician would concern himself with protection of the state from foreign threats, and the King would administer the internal affairs of the realm. It was strongly implied by the Chief Advisor that neither should meddle in the bailiwick of the other. Having arrived at an understanding entirely satisfactory to both, the King and the Sorcerer shook hands warmly and emerged from the vine-covered cottage arm in arm, the picture of solid friendship and eternal goodwill.

The Prince cried to leave his new friend. As the royal party mounted to embark on the long journey back to the castle, more than one retainer thought he saw a tear likewise glistening in the Sorcerer's eye, though whether it arose from the sadness of parting or from some other hidden melancholy, no one could determine.

CHAPTER THREE

The Prince Comes of Age

L ike ripe grain the days fell before the relentlessly swinging scythe of time, seemingly in bunches, but actually one by one, the hours, minutes, and seconds clinging like fat seeds to the head of each golden stalk. The harvested days were bundled together into weeks, and the sheaves were leaned together as months, until entire years stood stacked and yellowing in a regular pattern that receded into the distance and out of sight across the rolling countryside.

And the harvests were good in the kingdom of Nod, year after year. A sweet, bloated peace settled like a sigh upon the land. An entire generation of children, born of corpulent store clerks and fat-bellied farmers, knew nothing of the scourge of hunger nor the paralyzing threat of foreign invasion. They seemed to have been sired by a race of giants who possessed an unlimited capacity to provide and protect. These same farmers and merchants, themselves little educated, found the time and the money now to send a favorite son or daughter off for a year or two of schooling, and the University of Nod flourished. Church pews throughout the realm were packed each Sabbath with content, comfortable, and thankful citizens.

Outside the borders to the south and east, ragged hordes of moral dwarfs robbed, raped, pillaged, murdered, and performed infamous crimes against nature in an endless orgy of wickedness and evil. But no one in Nod cared any longer, for none of the barbarians dared to set foot within the kingdom, so awesome had the tales of the Sorcerer's terrible powers grown with the passing years.

The Sorcerer himself was seldom seen. Occasional reported sightings were doubtless apocryphal, inventions of the overtaxed imagination of a bookkeeper or the conjurings of a wistful fisherman's fancy. But signs of his presence were well known. Mysterious bursts of colored fire could be seen from time to time glowing just above the magician's mountain home, amidst monstrous rumblings that seemed to shake the earth's very core. These ominous reminders made as strong an impression upon the local populace as it did upon their foreign enemies. For the rascal with a penchant for criminal enterprise, a mere whisper of the wizard's terrible justice straightened a potentially crooked path. Mothers warned a wayward lad or lass to behave lest the Protector of the Kingdom discover the mischief and exact an unkind retribution. A fulsome variety of painful and embarrassing indignities, from spilt milk and moth holes to acid indigestion and hemorrhoids, were quietly attributed to the Sorcerer's mysterious powers and purposes.

Thanks to the Protector of the Kingdom, the army was no longer needed for the awkward and distasteful task of national defense. Public funds were channeled away from the militia. Occasionally the King would still review the troops, for form's sake, but in order to fill the small parade grounds, aging veterans would have to be called out of retirement to supplement the dwindling ranks. The once merely small army slowly deteriorated into an inept honor society for toothless old generals and assorted societal misfits. Its sole remaining role was to amuse the King and garnish his royal extravaganzas.

The King's reign was as unlike his father's as night is from day. He had revered, admired, loved, and secretly hated his father, never once suspecting that they were both driven by the same neurotic insecurity. The Old King had plunged into activity, leading military campaigns, endlessly touring the kingdom, overseeing public works projects, supervising local government, and maintaining political support with the ruthless determination of a desperado. The King avoided life as best he could. Nothing frightened him more than the unexpected, the little vicissitudes of life, the trials and tribulations which might spring up unannounced and reveal to all the world his fundamental inadequacy as a king and as a human being. In truth, he was inept at everything, because he had never in his life attempted anything.

Life had offered the King a single chance to blossom, and then had pruned it away again just as his spirit was beginning to bud. Three years before his death, the King's father had confronted his own mortality, concluded that lineal descendants might help matters, and arranged a marriage for his son with the beautiful young daughter of a rich silk merchant. Though she was fifteen years the King's junior, she possessed a genius for drawing the King out, building his confidence, and interesting him in the marvelous little activities of ordinary life. For more than a year life had been sweeter than he had ever dared to hope. On the evening the Prince was born, the King was the proudest man on the face of the earth. He tenderly kissed his beloved bride as she drifted off into a well-deserved sleep, a sleep from which she never awoke. She quietly died of internal hemorrhaging that night.

The King never trusted life again.

Yet it would be inaccurate to say he was unhappy as the years passed him by. The royal coffers were filled to overflowing from the exorbitant taxes on every possible human endeavor which the Old King had established when times were lean. Abundance mushroomed within the realm. The King could hardly spend money fast enough to keep up. He had long ago turned over the mundane details of running the kingdom to ministers he seldom saw, and comfort had totally extinguished any spark of ingenuity which may once have smouldered in the backwoods of his otherwise mediocre mind. He spent his time devising ever more elaborate, pompous, and expensive rituals for his daily court procedures, gathering his cronies about him like trained pigeons in splendid and absurd costumes, and buffering himself from the unanticipated. Those ceremonies which amused him, he repeated over and over again, until some of the younger attendants would grow embarrassed and look away, whispering that the King and his Chief Advisor were like two peas in a pod.

In sad fact, the passing years had not been kind to Grimm. He had grown quite senile, often confusing the King with his father whom he had served years ago, and mistaking the fuzzy past with the even fuzzier present. It was rumored that he suffered the insane delusion that God was whispering important messages into his left ear.

Occasionally he would be visited with brief flashes of lucidity, though they seemed to come with decreasing frequency, as if the old man fought them off, preferring instead to swim in the murky waters of muddled thinking. Perhaps in those rare and cruel instants of clarity the once-brilliant Chief Advisor had no choice but to face what he had become: a broken-down, drooling, humorless, smelly, white-haired, irrelevant old scutter.

Yet the King kept him on. Grimm would spend most of the day snoring quietly, asleep in the low chair reserved for him just below the King's right elbow, his tousled hair and bushy eyebrows white as freshly fallen snow upon the heap of his shrunken skin, so loose and shriveled that it seemed to have been torn off and abandoned by a disgruntled grizzly bear. Some said the King put up with him out of the goodness of his royal heart, as a gesture to all the old, the poor, the demented, the sick, and the halt, or at least for the sake of appearance, in deference to the venerable citizens of the realm who could recall Grimm's proud counsel when the Old King had been helmsman of the sea-tossed ship of state. Others suggested that the King himself was a little soft in the mind, and Grimm was the only member of his cabinet who spoke the same language.

In all the inner circles of the royal administration, the only unflickering flame seemed to be the young Prince as he grew older and ever bolder. More and more the King would rely upon his son to supervise at functions and preside at ceremonies, at first only in the remote outlands of the realm, but later whenever sovereign representation was called for outside the four walls of the castle. The King simply would not be bothered to travel abroad. The subjects came to know the Prince better than they did the King. The Prince became a symbol for the new enlightened self-sufficiency the kingdom now enjoyed. With the Prince as heir apparent to the throne, peace, prosperity, and a gentle rule of reason seemed assured for generations to come.

The Prince was the darling of the realm, and the citizens seemed unable to get enough of him. Young apprentices and clerks, without exception polite and pleasant fellows, if a little dull, would have sold their own parents into slavery to possess the spark of vivacity that flashed from his pale green eyes and sizzled within the words he spoke. Female hearts would go a-pitter-patter whenever the auburn-haired Prince appeared in public to cut the ribbon for a new irrigation dam, officially initiate a diversion canal, or dedicate a freshly completed monument to the living memory of the King. Many a housewife wept silently just to watch him ride past astride his chestnut stallion, shoulders thrown back, head held proudly, in command of a crack honor guard of haughty young horsemen.

Within the castle, downy daughters of staid and stuffy statesmen would catch the Prince's hand as they passed in the narrow mustiness of the royal cloakroom and whisper to him of a midnight tryst. And, indeed, the Prince was no stranger to matters of venereal delight, though no lovely lass had yet snared his fancy for longer than a momentary indiscretion. Except for his dreams, alas, true love itself had not so much as left him its calling card.

The Prince was a product of his age of plenty, representative of his generation, only somehow more so, as if his typical landscape had been painted in vivid colors by a more passionate hand. As a boy, he had been given everything his little heart desired, every new game, toy, pastime, or diversion the empire had to offer. In school he rose to the ninety-seventh percentile of his class overall. Later he took to competitive sports with an intensity that delighted his coaches and staggered his opponents. He seemed to have everything a young prince could possibly want.

One would suppose the Prince happy. But inside he was ravaged by unquenchable desires. Though he did very, very well at everything he attempted, he never quite managed to become the absolute best at anything. He raged after the elusive goal of perfection and resented those who finished ahead of him. A bitter discontent grew within him like a fetus, conceived of a ravenous curiosity, nurtured by unruly emotions, and aching to be born. Try though he might, it would not be aborted.

One day shortly after his eighteenth birthday, the Prince sought an audience with the King, who had just completed Royal Decrees and was about to begin Imperial Proclamations. Several attendants stood by in chartreuse leotards with epaulets of flocked juniper branches, and Grimm was snoozing in the Chief Advisor's chair. "Father," he said, "I am not happy."

"Oh, that doth sorrow us greatly." More and more of late the King tended to lapse into the regal first person plural even with his son. "Perhaps you would like a new jumping horse or a deer hide shuttleball." He gracefully raised his jeweled arm to summon the royal purser to count out enough money for the suggested purchases.

"No," the Prince interrupted. "That is not what I meant at all. That is not it at all."

The King lowered his arm, leaned closer, and squinted suspiciously, as if seeing his son for the first time in years. Where he had expected to find an angular, awkward, unkempt young rascal, a handsome prince now stood. "My, my, but you've grown, my boy. What seems to be the problem?"

"I'm being smothered, father, by all the sports and games and toys and schooling and endless imperial proceedings." The Prince's voice was full of emotion. "They're all distractions, and nothing more. It's all too comfortable, too predictable, and the distractions and the comfort keep me from reaching the truth."

The Prince now had his father's undivided attention. The King fidgeted uncomfortably. "But what are you looking for, my boy?"

"Well . . . truth. You know. I feel an emptiness inside. I hunger for knowledge of the true nature of things. Why, for example, am I here? What's my purpose?"

"Why to be king after me!" the King proclaimed proudly, pounding the back of the Chief Advisor's chair for emphasis.

Grimm straightened up, rubbed his eyes, and yawned.

"But why are there kings at all, father? I want to be absolutely certain that life on earth serves some purpose, because until I know that for certain, I will be discontented." The Prince searched his father's eyes for a glimmer of understanding. "Why, father, is there anything at all and not rather nothing?"

Jarred momentarily from its usual thought processes, the sovereign mind attempted to wrestle with the unfamiliar. "Ah, ah, ah," was all the King could manage to answer as he pondered the larger question. His eyes darted about for help.

"What does he want?" Grimm wanted to know, his voice shrill from paranoia. Having just awakened, he was a bit more muddled than usual. "What's he asking?"

"He wants to know the purpose of life," the King shouted irritably, as if sheer volume would render his words easier to comprehend. "Do you know what it is?"

Grimm rubbed his hoary pate with one hand and fumbled with his wizened genitals with the other. "Is it a trick?" he responded, much too loudly.

"Go back to sleep," the King snapped. "We'll take care of this."

"Might I suggest," whispered the nearest of the festooned attendants, perceiving the King's distress and trying to fill the void left by the Chief Advisor's incompetence, "that you could perhaps send him to the learned Professor Thatch."

"Of course!" cried the King, enormously relieved. "We shall send you to the learned Professor Thatch, my boy! He's head of the Department of Philosophy, Psychology, and Truth at the University of Nod. Perhaps you know of him? He'll certainly be able to help you."

"Thank you, father," said the Prince, bowing formally and retiring in the proper manner. With excitement and anticipation he put his affairs in order and packed for the journey to Enoch, where the University of Nod was located. He put aside the things of his youth and prepared himself, as best he could, for initiation into the world of higher learning.

CHAPTER FOUR

At the University

Enoch was the first city in the land of Nod, established by a venerable ancestor of the southern nomads. For many years it served as the capital of the realm. But repeated flooding from the River Enoch had destroyed the ancient city time and again until the King's great-grandfather had had enough. He removed the capital to the small southern village which had been his birthplace. The new capital had taken root and flourished. The antique brick and stone edifices of the once-vibrant city of Enoch now rose as forlornly as mausolea at the north end of the great Enoch Valley.

The Prince and his royal cortege rode north on the main highway toward Enoch. At the end of the second day they camped on the western slopes of the Sorcerer's mountain. A narrow, overgrown trail led away from the main road and wound out of sight up the steep slopes. The Prince took a walk by himself a little way up the trail after dinner. *Someday*, he thought, *I would like to meet the Sorcerer and learn from him.*

The night was warm and still, so the Prince lay outside under a veil of mosquito netting, pondering the series of accidents that were his life. As he lay thus awake, the full moon rose from behind the imposing mountain. For a moment the crest was a black silhouette haloed by the blazing lunar circle, and just before drifting off to sleep the Prince saw, or thought he saw, the dark outline of two figures standing there above, the wizard and another slender form, watching over his party and the entire kingdom, bestowing peace across the realm.

As they rode on northward the next day, the Prince glanced over his shoulder at the mountain peak. He had been but a young child when his father had taken him up that mountainside to personally bestow the honor of Protector of the Kingdom upon the wizard with an obsequiousness he had never again witnessed in the King. The memory stuck hard and unmoving in the jawbone of his very earliest recollections like an imaginary kernel between two thought molars.

It was hot on the afternoon of the third day when the Prince and his party arrived at the University of Nod. The campus was draped over the parched foothills to the southeast of Enoch like a cool green shawl. Fountains pulsed and splashed, lawn sprinklers tzat-tzat-tzatted, and a little creek gurgled pensively through the middle of that oasis of learning. The travelers were glad to have arrived.

"I shall not seek to leave this place," the Prince said to himself as he looked around, "until I have grasped the very essence of truth."

The Prince quickly enrolled in classes for philosophy, literature, science, and psychology. He purchased an armload of heavy books. To counterbalance his incorporeal pursuits, he also registered in the renowned Lamech College of Water Sports, where he learned from Lamech's venerable son himself the incredible and secret techniques of water-treading for which he had become so famous. A useful tool, the Prince thought to himself, for one studying near a city so prone to flooding.

But it was from Professor Thatch that the Prince hoped to receive the answers to his most profound inquiries. For his part, the good professor embraced his task of teaching the Crown Prince with honor, enthusiasm, and tenacity. He invited the Prince to stay with him at his own home, an ivy-covered cottage in a gopherwood glade adjoining the campus to the south. Long hours the two spent together probing the complexities of philosophy and psychological theories of knowledge.

The Prince applied himself with great diligence. He learned the precept that this world is only one of Becoming, an imperfect reflection of the timeless, absolute, and perfect Forms of Being. And as the Prince sat in the professor's kitchen, neat and orderly as a pine cone, he wondered how anyone could know of Forms that were outside the possible realm of worldly experience. So Professor Thatch taught him the teachings of more recent thinkers, that the rational was the real and the real was the rational. In amazement the Prince rolled, like a cerebral mint on the mind's tongue, the concept of reducing all reality to the syllogistic unfolding of rational thought. He learned that underlying the universe was perfect order, the scientific precision and mathematical exactness of space and time, cause and effect, and the irrefutable, hierarchical, and inescapable laws of nature.

In wonder the Prince asked his mentor, "Does this include me too? Am I bound to be played like an organ stop by the orderly hand of nature? Have I no free will?"

So Professor Thatch taught him of ethical considerations for use in the crystal palace of logic. The Prince tossed and turned in his dogmatic slumber as he grew acquainted with the categorical imperative: that the only truly good will comes from acting in such a manner that every action could be made a universal principle of conduct for all men. And the Prince looked over his own life and saw that his actions had never yet flowed freely forth from the pure fountainheads of reason and logic, but had churned and gurgled up passionately from a wellspring of dark necessity deep within him, and he knew not why or how.

The Prince was sorely troubled. The more he understood of philosophy, the less it seemed to be able to account for the chaotic reality of his own life. He needed something more to explain himself. He yearned to touch that nameless primordial force lying just beyond reason, for which philosophy could not account, to grasp it and make it his, to conquer and control it. Without it the other teachings seemed hollow.

Professor Thatch's daughter was two years younger than the Prince. The two of them would study together, analyzing the "chairness" of chairs, comparing apples and oranges, and puzzling over the sound of a tree falling in the woods when no one was around to hear it. She was a slight, anemic young woman with mousy brown hair and small, high, girlish breasts, which the Prince, try as he might to keep his mind on philosophical truths and his actions within the bounds of reason, longed to cup in his moist palms.

They would sit late at the dining room table, side by side, long after the dishes had been cleared away and washed and the professor had retired, reflecting upon the natural order of the universe, while within him the Prince knew only disorder. The slight warm pressure of her leg against his thigh as they sat reading epistemological treatises rose like molten lava within his loins, flooding reason, inundating distinctions, deluging abstractions, until one evening during the third month of his tenure, he discovered his hand had found its way to her thigh, as if nothing out of the ordinary were happening, then to her trembling belly, and when she did not resist, and, in fact, continued to speak of qualitative analytical distinctions which had long ago become meaningless rainfall upon the umbrellaed ears of his intellect, to those small, warm, quivering jelly-breasts he so distractingly craved.

So much for the study of philosophy. For the remainder of the term they would languish after dinner, counting hours bloated by distended minutes and corpulent seconds, waiting for Professor Thatch to retire, as he did each evening at precisely 9:15. Then they would enter together the sacred carnal library, opening and devouring the pink volume of each other's body for the only knowledge that seemed to satisfy. Oh, scholarships and cum laude degrees aplenty they would have won, these two honor students of the flesh, had they been graded on their nocturnal inquiries, sublunary probings, and midnight musings, ending as they would just at daybreak, tantalizingly ever nearer to the hour the professor would arise, punctual as a clock-work cuckoo, to declare the reestablishment of the reign of reason.

Alas, the Prince's already waning enthusiasm for philosophy flagged altogether. His essay exams were turned in full of blank, white pages. His multiple-choice quizzes came back looking like tic-tac-toe scorecards. His riotous thoughts would break out of the corral of right-thinking and refused to be lassoed and branded in the cerebral roundup. In class he would daydream when he was able to stay awake at all. No one dared criticize him. His life settled down into the track of comfort which was fast wearing into a rut. He began to feel that he was wasting his time. Even the professor's daughter grew annoying, in the daylight pretending to discuss irrelevant doctrines of utility, dualism, and the scientific method, and at night prodding his privates when he wished only to sleep away the wearisome world of higher learning. The Prince found himself caught in a bind, lost between lust and learning, and both directions seemed to lead him away from his quest for the truth.

"Surely I have taken a wrong turn somewhere along the road to truth," the Prince muttered one morning at the breakfast table, balancing his copy of *Ethical Inquiries* on the blade of his butter knife.

"What did you say?" Professor Thatch asked, repairing the irregular surfaces of his muffin with a grape jelly patch.

"Oh, I don't know." The Prince glanced absently from the professor to his unremarkable daughter seated breathlessly beside him at the table. He allowed the axiology volume to flatten the knife and wiped his hands on his napkin. "I came here looking for something, and now I'm convinced that this isn't the place where it is to be found."

"Precisely what do you seek?" the professor asked.

"I wish to see clearly what I am and why I'm here at all. I want to know with absolute certainty that there's a purpose to the apparently random confusion of everyday life. What's *my* purpose?"

"I see." Professor Thatch laid down his muffin. "Philosophy is a science, and as a science, it deals with possibilities. By observation and discursive thinking we approach probabilities, and from them we interpolate principles as best we can. It's all subject to refinement, amendment, and even contradiction if the observations or the reasoning so dictate. But truth, no. Philosophy can never give you the absolute certainty you crave."

"If the answers cannot be found in philosophy," the Prince replied, "then I must look elsewhere."

The professor's pale daughter grew even paler. She opened her trembling mouth to say something, but no sound came out.

"Your affliction is spiritual, not intellectual," the professor rejoined. He picked up the muffin and took a bite, ruminating on both muffin and the spiritual dilemma. He failed to notice the tears in his daughter's eyes as she fled the table without a word. "Might I suggest that you seek out a spiritual leader of some sort? A mystical master who has himself come to grips with your inquiry and who has surmounted it. Such a one would be able to guide you far better than I."

So that very morning the royal cavalcade mounted for the long return to the castle. "I'm sorry," was all the Prince could say at his valediction.

Professor Thatch in his turn apologized for the unexpected absence of his daughter. "She's unaccountably taken ill with fits of fainting," he explained. "No doubt it's caused by those queer spells the Sorcerer's been casting lately."

"You have returned before the term's end, my son," the King remarked as he watched two brightly costumed attendants escort the Chief Advisor toward a small doorway on the opposite side of the throne room. Grimm had accidentally befouled himself a few moments earlier as he sat dozing beside the King, and the attendants were half carrying, half dragging the old man out, trying to take him to the washroom to clean him up. But now that the Prince had entered the chamber, Grimm began to resist rabidly, as if it were of the utmost importance that he attend the impending interview.

The aroma of Grimm's mishap hung uneasily in the air, and the remaining attendants shifted self-consciously at their ceremonial stations by the throne. The King turned to his son. "And did you find the answers you were seeking with the help of Professor Thatch?"

"No, father. I am sorry."

The King's smile flitted from his face like a skittish butterfly into a balmy summer breeze. "Oh my, and are you still troubled?"

"Yes, father."

"Did this Thatch fellow refuse to help you?" The King's right hand tightened around the royal mace.

"No, father," the Prince interceded. "He was in fact most energetic and helpful. It's just . . . well . . . his philosophy is spiritually . . . empty. It all seems so . . . irrelevant."

The King relaxed, beaming once again to see that the royal blood indeed coursed through the veins of the Prince, allowing him to pass callous judgment upon the lives of his subjects as offhandedly as the King himself had long ago learned to do.

Suddenly a piercing, shrill, mewing scream like the shriek of a dozen tormented banshees, an unearthly sound that until that very moment had been widely considered unutterable by the human tongue, tore from between Grimm's foam-speckled, snarling lips as the smaller of the two attendants began pealing his white-knuckled fingers, one by one, from the edge of the ornate cornice framing the small doorway. The squawking achieved its crescendo as the attendants finally managed to pry the Chief Advisor loose and stuff him, flailing, through the narrow doorway, one of them losing his feathered, three-cornered headpiece in the process. Everyone breathed easier when the little door was finally shut behind them.

"Grimm seems to want to stay," the Prince observed.

"He has a suggestion to offer you, my son."

"Oh?" The Prince was mildly apprehensive. "Is this a direct communication from God?"

"He didn't say."

"What does he advise?"

"Grimm suggests that perhaps it's time," the King said slowly, as if wisely, "you studied with Father Constant. The Church of Nod will surely have answers for your deepest questions."

The suggestion seemed surprisingly sound to the Prince.

The King leaned forward and in an uncharacteristic moment of regal insight added in a lower voice, "And it's time a trusted representative of the Crown paid a long-overdue visit to the inner sanctum of the Church. To examine its most private workings, eh?"

"Yes, father." The Prince was dutifully obedient as he had been trained and curiously excited at the prospect of this new challenge.

CHAPTER FIVE

The Church of Nod

At the southeast corner of the realm, just below the high pass that led to the uncivilized mountainous regions beyond, the Monastery of the Church of Nod lay forebodingly across a narrow saddle of rock between ragged granite cliff faces like a whalebone caught in the maw of the Earth Giant. Antique stone walls and low brooding clouds endowed the structure with a grave and sinister aspect as the Prince and his entourage approached along the road that wound through the ragged foothills from the west.

A young monk in a hooded cloak pushed open the massive door in the moss-covered stone wall and, without uttering a word, motioned for the royal party to pass through. Their silent guide repeated the ceremony at a second gate in an inner, lower wall which the cavalcade came to shortly. The Prince and his retinue were then guided through a twisting canyon of ancient stone block until they came to yet another wall and another gate. Here the somber monk rang a huge bell, bowed once, and returned along the way they had come.

The gate was opened from the other side and a middle-aged monk stepped out. He was attired in a burnoose of rough brown, hand-sewn wool. "I am Brother Widgeon, and I shall accompany you the rest of the way to Father Constant, your highness." He bowed deeply. "The rest of your company will not be allowed beyond this point, I am afraid."

The Prince was startled by this abrupt order that purported to tell him, the Crown Prince of Nod, who could or could not accompany him further. But wishing to avoid a confrontation so early in his stay, he allowed the matter to pass. He nodded to the monk. "Proceed. I will follow you alone." He gestured to his chief attendant to stay behind with the assorted porters, attendants, swordsmen, archers, and unclassified retainers. "I trust my party will find adequate accommodations during the course of my stay."

"I will see to it personally as soon as I return," the monk assured him.

The pathway through the winding narrow inner streets, guarded gateways, and twisting cloistered corridors was labyrinthine indeed. Although the Prince quickly lost his bearings, Brother Widgeon seemed to know the way well. As they spiraled their way into the heart of the monastery, the mood of the architecture, which had been depressingly somber and ascetic, grew ever more elaborate, ornate, bright, and polished. The rooms they passed by were ever more elegantly appointed, with furniture of richly worked wood inlaid with silver and gold accent.

At last Brother Widgeon stopped before a huge, finely-carved door, picked up an exquisite silver chime from the table nearby, and rang three times, bowing deeply after each ring. Immediately the door opened, and a short, square man with thinning hair, a robust, ruddy face, and a jovial, beatific, white-enamel smile of perfect teeth stepped out. He beamed at the Prince, threw open his arms as if embracing the whole world, and bellowed, "Welcome!"

At first the Prince did not recognize Father Constant without his crimson robes and pontifical cap. He seemed absurdly short compared to the Prince's recollection of the few times, long ago, he had seen the high priest performing religious ceremonies in and about the castle. This man wore a plain pair of dark, baggy pants and a dazzling white shirt, clean but badly wrinkled, the sleeves rolled up to the elbow. Even Professor Thatch had been more elegantly tailored.

"Come in, come in," crooned the Prelate, slipping his arm easily around the Prince's shoulders and ushering him through the doorway. Brother Widgeon was ignored and forgotten. "I have looked forward to this meeting for days, ever since I first received word that you would be studying with us." He exploded in a hearty laugh. "What a wonderful chance this will be to cement relations between the Church of Nod and the Crown. I must frankly admit," he continued, his countenance suddenly twisted into an unaccustomed scowl, "that such relations have been deteriorating a bit in the past few years." The dark thought passed and his smile seemed to spring back by itself. "Ah, your father and I had such hopes for this kingdom when we were in school together. Alas, we rarely communicate any longer. But that's all going to change with your visit, don't you think?" Then as if seeing the Prince for the first time, "My goodness, how you've grown, my boy!"

"It's a pleasure to be here, your Grace," the Prince replied properly, glancing about the comfortable room.

"Oh, there's no need for such formalities as 'your Grace.' We're all friends here. We'll need to cut through all these rituals and ceremonies if we really hope to understand each other's position, wouldn't you agree? Do you like my study? I find it quite comfortable and an absolute necessity when I want to get any work done. I simply can no longer work at home. My wife and my daughter–"

"Wife and daughter!"

"Yes, my boy, of course. Please don't look so shocked. You'll meet them this very evening, and surely you would prefer to stay at my house, rather than shivering all night on a cold stone pallet with the neophyte monks. You're royalty! No need for you to suffer just to take in a little religious training."

"But priests are supposed to be celibate," the Prince objected.

"Oh, *that*. Well, certainly, that's the story we like to tell, and of course it's the image of the clergy we want to maintain. And it does represent the rules of the monastery, but . . ."

The Prince's puzzlement showed in spite of his attempt to maintain composure and good manners.

"Oh, don't take it so seriously," the Prelate laughed, clapping the Prince on the back. "Hell's bells, boy, the rule of celibacy isn't carved in bedrock. It's not in God's ordinance. You won't find it in the scriptures. It's just a little something the high council made up a few years ago to get a leg up on the masses with all their whoring, wife swapping, and perversion. And I still think it was a good idea, don't you? But this celibacy business comes from our own house rules, and rules are made to be broken, aren't they? If you have to break some rules, what's safer than breaking a few that you made up yourself?" He leaned closer. "Frankly, there's a whole lot of show business in religion, and we're going to let you see how it's all done, the inside working, nothing held back. But this will all be just between you and me. And the King, of course. Agreed?"

The Prince nodded.

"Now suppose you tell me what in the world ever made you want to come to the monastery yourself? What is it you'd like to learn about us while you're here?"

The Prince began to relate to Father Constant his confusion about finding his place and purpose in life. As he rambled on, the High Priest straightened several books in his bookcase and tidied up his desk a bit. The Prince could not tell if he was listening.

"Oh, my gosh!" the Prelate exclaimed suddenly, interrupting the Prince's brief soliloquy. "Dinner's in five minutes. We'd better leave the monastery right now and get home or there'll be hell to pay."

"But it takes twenty minutes just to get back to the main gate," the Prince protested, rising.

"'Tis only an illusion, my boy, like so many others in this business." Father Constant slipped on a faded brown dinner jacket. "Come on, this door opens out through the wall of the monastery to a little group of houses up above, where the families and . . . er . . . shall we say 'friends' of some of the upper-order priests live." He opened a door in the back wall of the study and hustled the Prince through.

"But what of all the streets and corridors and gates and walls that Brother Widgeon took me through to get here in the first place?"

"An illusion, my boy," the Prelate replied, leading him down a short passageway and out into an open street lined with quaint single-story cottages beneath a brooding sky. "Poor Widgeon, bless his soul, still hasn't figured it all out yet. Not too bright, poor chap, but a hard worker and as devout as they come. I'm afraid he'd be quite disappointed if he were ever to find out."

At the end of the next block stood one house grander than the others. As they started up the walkway, Father Constant took the Prince by the arm and stopped him for a moment. "While you and I are exploring matters of the spirit and improving relations between

Church and Crown, I've instructed my housemaid Myrnah to look after your corporal needs." He winked at the Prince. Then as they continued on to the front door he added, "I trust you'll convey to the King how well you've been treated while you're here."

And well treated indeed he was. That first supper was resplendently laid out in great abundance. Fine wine flowed freely, though the Prince drank little. Myrnah hovered to attend his every need or want. Her hair was long and reddish-brown, pinned up above a lovely face, ruddy as fine ripe fruit, with flashing eyes and a quick smile. Lithe and graceful she was, yet buxom in all the right places. The Prince found pleasant distraction watching her glide about her duties.

After brandy with the Prelate, the Prince begged off on offers of further entertainment, for he was tired from the long day's ride. Myrnah led him up the stairs to a fine suite of cosy rooms that would be his place of repose. A fire crackled in the small fireplace. He settled into a comfortable chair beside the warming glow. Without bidding, Myrnah turned up the oil lamp and asked, "Would ye take a nice cup'o' chamomile tea a'fore y'retire, m'Lord?"

"Thank you, Myrnah, that would be fine. I think I'll just glance through this little book Father Constant has given me." He couldn't help watch her slip gracefully through the doorway, then lowered his eyes to consider the *Novice's Guide to the Ancient Mysteries, Part I*.

On the very first page the small volume announced what it called "The Most Overlooked Truth in the World," namely, that the Holy Scripture contains the Word of God. The absolute, complete, and irrefutable truth. Not a single word can be questioned, for the entire Scripture holds together as an intricate and magnificent edifice of revelation. He who can master the Holy Scripture shall have his every question answered and his every need fulfilled.

The Prince had never given much thought to God, having never been called upon to do so at the palace. The concept seemed a bit odd. Nonetheless, the promises of the little book were intriguing.

On bare feet Myrnah padded in softly and set a cup of hot tea and plate of scones on the low table between his chair and the fire.

She stood watching him silently until he glanced up from his studies. She had changed into a light beige cotton shift that clung to her body. Her long auburn tresses had been unbound and now spilled over her shoulders and down her back.

Ah, he thought, *a comely lass. A forbidden distraction, alas. Too bad.*

"Will ye be retiring soon, m'Lord?"

"Yes, Myrnah, in a few minutes."

"Then I'll just turn down your bed for ye." She spun on slender ankles.

"Ah . . . fine. Thank you." He sipped his tea and forced his attention back to the promising little volume.

"And, by your leave," she added, poking her head out of the bed chamber, "warm it up a bit for ye. 'Tis a frosty night."

"As you will," he muttered absently. "Good night."

These scriptures seemed to offer him the root of all spiritual meaning. Could they provide the answers that had been eluding him like quicksilver for so long? His mind harbored doubt. But what little would it cost him to suspend his incredulity for a while and surrender to the spiritual path? To follow this path a ways, to see where it lead? He read on about prayer and fasting, silence and meditation, and ceremonies of purification.

A deep yawn racked his body. The Prince reached for his cup, but the tea had grown cold. In the hearth the ghost of a fitful blue flame danced above a few bright embers. He yawned again and laid the volume aside, stretched his arms, rolled his shoulders, and blew out the reading lantern. The room was plunged into darkness, but for the red glow of the fireplace and a single slim taper guttering dimly within a cut-glass vase. He drew back the drape and carried the candle into his sleeping chamber, where the Prince removed his clothing. Orienting himself, he blew out the candle, padded to the bedside, and swung his legs up beneath the comforter.

"*Ayee!*" he cried, recoiling. "*What devilry is this?*"

Another body lay in his bed.

"Oh, my Lord!" came Myrnah's frightened reply. "I beg your forgiveness! 'Twas my wretched misunderstanding."

The Prince reached out and felt the soft roundness of her naked flesh.

"I'll away at once," she sobbed, rising to crawl over him.

"Shhh," comforted the Prince, enclosing her in a reassuring embrace.

"Woulds't thou not have me leave?"

"Shhh," he repeated, pressing his fingers to her lips. For a long time he held her close until the trembling subsided. Gradually her silken touch kindled those primordial flames deep within him which, soon raging out of control, consumed them both. She took him like a warm, wet melon freshly broken open, slippery, bottomless, and sweet. Afterwards he fell into a deep sleep, and when he awoke early the next morning, she was gone, leaving behind the sticky warm aroma of animals rutting in a musty burrow.

The Prince attended his first classes of religious instruction not as a novice, sitting painfully cross-legged on the cold stone floor, but as a visiting dignitary, privy to all the pontifical secrets and deserving of all honors. He was never called upon nor asked to participate in the frequent tests, exercises, or recitations which the neophytes undertook. As the day wore on, the Prince began to feel that he was not seeing the monastery as it really was, but an elaborate production put on specially in his honor.

On the second night the Prince found Myrnah warming his bed once again, and though from the spiritual standpoint he found this distraction annoying, yet in his heart her charms were hard to resist. And on the night after that the scene was repeated with the relentless precision of the industrial production of fine surgical instruments. The Prince quickly lost track of any difference in his sequential encounters with her, as if the nights had been telescoped into a single frenzied encounter.

With the dawn of the fourth morning, the sun's bright lance pierced the everlasting fog and brought a new lucidity to the Prince. He had come hence with a clear purpose, and now found himself hopelessly adrift and rudderless in a social game as convoluted and distracting as that of the palace. He had not journeyed all this way for dalliances and indulgences. He felt put upon, the victim of some baleful plan, an actor in a complex theatrical production who had been given only a small part of the script to read. So he decided to rewrite the script altogether.

As they trudged through the crisp morning sunlight toward the monastery, he informed Father Constant of his intent. "I came here to learn the substance of your discipline, and yet I'm being treated like a guest of state. Distractions are heaped into my path. I don't believe I'm really learning the marrow of your teachings."

"You are an honored guest," the Prelate grinned. "We wouldn't want your stay to be unpleasant. What you're learning goes far beyond what the other trainees are offered."

"Let me decide that," snapped the Prince, for the first time implying the supremacy of Crown over Church. "I wish to train as a neophyte monk for a while, then you and I can talk some more."

The cleric's smile had become a frozen mask. He was obviously troubled by the proposal, and yet could not ignore the cold edge of authority in the Prince's words, shining like a honed blade. "I . . . er . . . I'm sure that could be . . . er . . . arranged." He thought for a moment. His face brightened. "A neophyte needs a spiritual confident and counselor, however, as he makes his progress through our religious education. I will select an appropriate senior monk for your personal tutor and guide. I have just--"

"That won't be necessary," countered the Prince. "I've already selected one."

"And who might that be?" The churchman was apprehensive.

"Brother Widgeon."

Father Constant nodded wanly. "As you will, your majesty."

"And I'll be sleeping in the monastery from now on. Will you be kind enough to make the arrangements?"

The Prince's days as a neophyte were spent quite differently from those of his initial stay at the monastery. Up well before the dawn for prayer and recitation of scripture, he endured long hours of dreary lectures and endless reading, his legs and shoulders aching from the cold and formal positions of obeisance, servitude, and prayer. The course wool of the trainees' vestments scratched his neck until it was red and sore, and the meager meals of bread and watery oatmeal left him forever hungry. Like the others, he was forbidden to talk to anyone except his own personal counselor. Yet the Prince submitted without a word of protest, and a savage joy arose within his heart and carried him through the darkest hours. Never in his life had he experienced the incredible detachment that flowed from the lengthy attempts at silent, wordless prayer.

Brother Widgeon accepted his duty warmly, and he and the Prince became genuine friends, although the Prince was troubled that he already knew things about the reality behind the monastic life that his mentor did not even suspect. He rather hoped that the good man never suffered the torment of learning the truth.

With Brother Widgeon's guidance the Prince applied himself vigorously to the task of mastering the doctrines of the Church of Nod. He learned of the Creation and of man's Fall from Grace, of the power of the Evil One in the world, and some general rules on how to distinguish good from evil. He studied the abstract notions of God as the Unmoved Mover, the First Cause, and the Undifferentiated One. His classes included instruction in postures of prayer, church rituals, ministering to the congregation, and the proper preparation of acceptable meals. Scripture was presented to him as the revealed Word of God, transcribed by inspired men, and he learned the ideal of absolute obedience to the expressed Will of God. He studied religious symbols of power and the doctrines of God the Father and God the Holy Ghost. Ask, he was taught, and it shall be given, for the power of believing is power absolute.

At special Sunday services where Father Constant would dress up in his pontifical vestments, his crimson robes flowing and his gold-trimmed miter bobbing through the ceremony like a cork on a wave of divine revelation, the Prince witnessed the laying on of hands and the miraculous healing of the sick and lame right before his eyes. He was admonished to think only pure thoughts, cajoled to spread the word of God, and apprised to make constant war upon unbelievers and infidels, both within and without the borders of the kingdom. (This latter doctrine gave the Prince pause, and he made a mental note to discuss its implications with his father.)

And yet for all the serenity, peace, and calm the training

generated in his heart, doubt lay heavy upon the Prince's mind, like the fog that endlessly filled the great valley to the west. In an attempt to dispel it, he talked at length with Brother Widgeon. But the monk already had his faith secure and was unable to help the Prince get over the hurdle of believing in the first place. He would simply smile and tell the Prince, gently, "Believing comes first, and then everything else will fall into place." And the monk seemed so content, so at peace, so untroubled and blissful with his solid faith that the Prince was loathe to bring up some of the harsh inconsistencies and bald absurdities that seemed to him to haunt the fundamental teachings, lest by his own doubts he might infect the older man's beatitude.

One evening while the Prince was wrestling with what he conceived to be a patent inconsistency in the doctrine of evil, Brother Widgeon quietly entered the room and set down a small sheaf of papers on the edge of his desk.

"What's this?" the Prince wanted to know.

"These are to be inserted in your copy of the scriptures," the older monk explained. "The instruction sheet tells you where each sheet goes and what is to be taken out and discarded. I'm told there will be more in a few days."

The Prince stared at him blankly.

"These are revisions–"

"Revisions?"

"Yes."

"To the scriptures?"

"Yes, of course. You didn't think that God had abandoned us, did you?" Brother Widgeon smiled benevolently. "The Lord looks after his flock, and when further clarification or instruction is needed, he sends us revisions to the scriptures."

"Who writes these revisions?"

"Why, God-inspired men, of course. Men into whom God has breathed the truth."

"But who are they?" The Prince wanted very much to meet such men and talk with them. Perhaps they could help him to understand and believe. "Where are they?"

"Where?" The monk frowned. "I'm not really sure, actually."

His face brightened. "But I'm sure the head monk could tell you."

The Prince set out immediately in search of the head monk. He intercepted the man in the broad corridor leading from Father Constant's chambers. "Where are the revised scriptures being written?" he asked breathlessly. "I demand to know in the name of the Crown."

The wary old monk glanced around to see if anyone was watching. Then he jerked his thumb towards the Prelate's ornate door and scuttled on down the hallway.

The Prince knocked.

In a moment the door was drawn open a crack. When Father Constant recognized the Prince, he threw it open wide. "Welcome, come in, come in." The high priest seemed genuinely relieved to see him, ushered him inside, sat him down before a blazing fire, and poured them each a snifter of brandy. "I'm pleased that you have survived your ordeal with no serious injuries. At first I was a bit worried. Our program can be rigorous and unpleasant for those of us who are accustomed to a more genteel lifestyle." He lit a cigar and puffed it several times. "But then I remembered that you are indeed your father's son." He gestured a small toast at the reference to the King, and they both sipped to it. The churchman chuckled. "Yes, you are clever, like your father. I think I might have done just the same as you did. In order to really find the truth out about a place, one has to go behind the scenery and fanfare, no?"

The Prince glanced around the small chamber as the Prelate prattled. Sheets of paper lay scattered about upon almost ever surface, laid out in some intricate pattern whose purpose he could not discern. No one else was there. He took another sip of the fine liquor.

The Prince was obviously interested in the papers spread out around them, so after a thoughtful pause, Father Constant picked up several sheets lying on the table next to him and handed them to the younger man. "These are some scripture revisions which are almost finished."

The Prince took the sheets. Much of the text had been crossed out and interlineations scratched like footprints of a drunken spider. The subject was the nature of God's absolute prescience. "Ah," he said. "This is one of the topics that has given me some difficulty. Do you mind if I ask you a question or two?"

"Certainly not, my boy!" Father Constant chuckled again. "Now we shall interrogate the head of the Church before concluding our investigation, right? Fine! From the first moment you arrived I have been candid and open about our operations as could be. We have no secrets to hide here, especially from the King." He toasted the King once again. "To friendship, candor, and a strong alliance of mutual interests!"

The Prince sipped his brandy. "First of all, it seems to me that if God could indeed see the intricate detail of all future events at the time he created the world, then He is responsible for creating the evil as well as the good in the world. How can we worship such a God?"

"Evil was introduced not by God, but by man's abuse of his free will," the Prelate responded patly, pointing to some notes scrawled in the margin of one of the sheets the Prince was holding, and puffed his cigar.

"But that really doesn't resolve the matter," the Prince protested. "If free will is truly free, then God couldn't know from the first what was going to happen, could He? I'm afraid there's a fundamental inconsistency here somewhere."

"Right! Quite perceptive, my boy." Father Constant set down his snifter, leaned closer, and snatched the sheets gently from the Prince's grasp. "This is one of the tougher little nuts to crack." He scratched another note in the margin.

The Prince saw that the handwriting was the same. "Why, *you're* the one who's rewriting the sacred text!"

The Prelate looked up sheepishly. "You're on the mark there. It's one of our principal duties as priests, to gloss over these little scriptural embarrassments as best we can, no? Would you like to try your hand at it?"

"Writing scripture?!"

"Certainly. Someone has to write it, after all. I think a man of your intellect, in a dispassionate mood, might have a good shot at working out some of these nasty tangles."

"But the scriptures have been written by God-inspired men.

That's what you teach."

"And that's precisely why we're in this quagmire," the Prelate fumed, waving his cigar about, "rife with paradoxes, replete with logical inconsistencies, teeming with non sequiturs. A prophet drugged or drunk or hyped up on a delusional encounter with his Maker doesn't take the time to reason these things through properly, and we of the clergy have to step in and help him sort it all out into something consistent and believable."

The Prince's thoughts jumped to Grimm, the King's batty Chief Advisor, and the strange swimming instructor he had encountered at the university. Each believed that God had spoken to him personally. What kind of scripture were they capable of writing? What could the Prince expect to learn from them? He sighed and slumped deeper into the comfortable chair.

Father Constant carefully carved the ash from the tip of his cigar. "I've been toying with the idea of prophesying the coming of a personal savior in the indefinite future, to give the folks something to look forward to so they can better shoulder their present duty, painful though it sometimes is, and maintain the essential social order." He puffed on his cigar. "I had in mind a prophet, anointed by the Lord, say, to preach good tidings to the poor, to heal the brokenhearted, to free the spiritually fettered, and to proclaim the acceptable year of the Lord. Ask the King for me what he thinks of the idea, will you?"

The Prince shook his head in dismay.

Father Constant put his hand gently on the Prince's shoulder and smiled paternally. "I certainly hope you didn't take our teachings too literally. I was afraid you might when I learned of your enthusiasm. I'm truly sorry to disappoint you. But surely you know, as the Crown Prince, that religion is essential to the welfare of the kingdom. It's a tool for social engineering. The purpose of our Church of Nod is social order, and that's why an impeccable relationship between the Church and the Crown is essential. We're both in the same business at bottom, you see. We try to make religion mysterious, awesome, and yet believable, like that faith healing flimflam we put on every Sunday, in order to retain a certain amount of control over the masses.

To be used in conjunction with good government, of course. People without enough to eat or clothing for their families might cause social unrest, increase the general disorder, with the resulting spread of pain, starvation, and anarchy. If they're not kept in check by promises of justice in the afterlife, they might want their justice *now*."

The reasoning held a certain compelling fascination which the Prince could not ignore, yet he felt he had lost something of immeasurable importance in the instant just before he had really grasped it, and it made him sad.

"And while on the subject of order in the kingdom," the Prelate continued, "I would suggest that your father watch that so-called Sorcerer a bit closer. He's got tremendous influence on the imagination of the masses, and we have no control over *him*. The situation could easily get out of hand." He snuffed out the cigar and nodded. "A word to the wise." He stood up, then smiling again, poured them each another two fingers of brandy.

"I must return at once to the castle," declared the Prince abruptly, setting down his untouched brandy and arising.

"Ah, the investigation's over, is it?" beamed the Prelate. "I hope the report will be a favorable one." He clapped the Prince on the shoulder. "Remember, your father's ermine cape and these religious vestments are cut from the same cloth. Our only duty is to win full submission of the will of the masses. For their own good, of course. It's as simple as politics." Grinning, he clasped the Prince's hand warmly. "Do give my best to the King, won't you?"

CHAPTER SIX

The Sorcerer's Prescription

W hen the young Prince returned again to the grand throne room, as hungry as ever for an understanding of the true nature of reality, his father was in an uncharacteristically foul mood.   In order to settle a knotty child custody dispute between two contentious and uncompromising subjects, the King, following his Chief Advisor's sudden inspiration, had just ordered that an infant be sawed in half, and the screaming, the blood, gore, Grimm's violent retching, and the general hysteria had so completely unnerved him, that in a majestic rage he had banished Grimm from his sovereign presence. He swore to himself that it was high time the old gaffer was permanently put out to pasture. His rage had moderated somewhat, but the King still felt queasy in his stomach, and a king with a queasy stomach is a king to be avoided.

"Father?"

"Yes, what do you want now?" the King barked.

"Oh, I'm sorry." The Prince detected the direction the wind was blowing. "I can come back later."

"Don't tell me when you'll come and go around here! Are you still dwelling on that childish obsession of yours, boy? When I was your age, I was in the counting house learning to count the money. That's what you need, a job.   Get your mind off this crazy quest-for-truth tripe. How do you ever expect to manage the throne and dispense justice if your head is off somewhere in the clouds? Answer me that, boy!"

The Prince remained silent, for he perceived the question to be rhetorical.

"Philosophy doesn't do any good," the King began again like an intermittent fumarole. "Religion doesn't seem to take. What you need is to get your feet set on the solid ground. You act as if you're possessed by demons. Why, I have half a mind to send you to the Sorcerer for a stiff potion to purge you of evil spirits."

At the mention of the wizard, the Prince's ears perked. He had for these many years harbored a hidden enchantment for the man and his magical powers. Perhaps, he thought to himself, the Sorcerer is the one to help me! Perhaps he could give me the answers! But to his father he only said, "I will, of course, honor your wisdom and submit to your will, father."

"Yes," sputtered the King, calming. "Wisdom. Indeed, yes. Harrumph. Yes, that was a wise idea, was it not?" He looked around, and his attendants all nodded nervously. Forgetting his dyspepsia momentarily, the King smiled broadly. "Yes, indeed. And why not the Sorcerer? Indeed. We must tell him not to prescribe anything too drastic, of course, but . . . yes! I like the idea! A mild purgative might help to soothe your troubled heart, my son."

So like an errant boomerang, off again went the royal entourage, this time to the dwelling place of the Sorcerer of Nod, honorable Protector of the Kingdom. In accordance with the understanding between the King and the wizard reached many years ago, no one was to go unbidden into the Sorcerer's private mountain retreat, unless it was on official business from the King himself. And no one in the kingdom at large had set eyes on the wizard for half a generation, save for the King's messengers, and they were strictly forbidden by the King from discussing their visits. Once a year the King would send his greetings by high envoy on the anniversary of their momentous accord. Many people suggested that the King really just wanted to be sure the realm's Protector was still alive, in good health, and upholding his end of the bargain. In all the years, no other business had ever come up between the two men. Until now.

After two day's ride the royal cavalcade turned off the main highway that linked the capital with the city of Enoch to the north. Towering over them was the Sorcerer's mountain, and the Prince felt an unexpected thrill. Though he had passed this way on several occasions over the years, he had never ventured more than a short way along the brambly pathway that wound and twisted and switched back and forth up the face of the imposing mountainside.

As the procession made its slow way up the trail, the Prince recalled tales of the Sorcerer and his mountain which he had listened to avidly as a child, tales he had heard for as long as he could remember. Sometimes on moonless nights, it was told, when there was a strange stillness in the wind, dogs would howl wildly and then slink for cover beneath the buildings, trembling. On such a night, if a resident of one of the small villages which were scattered within view of the peak were to go outside (and few dared to go out on such a night), an eerie red halo could be seen glowing atop the Sorcerer's mountain like a nebulous golf ball, and a queer rumbling, so deep as to be almost inaudible, could be felt troubling the earth. Yes, on such a night the townspeople knew without having to be told that secret magical powers were being wrought and wielded, powers that were better left unknown, powers that could crush an army horribly and drive an ordinary man insane just by hearing them named.

The ascent took the better part of a day, with frequent rests for the lathered horses. When the party finally rode over the crest of the last hill, passed beneath a gigantic cypress, and dropped into the gentle valley rimmed by summit ridges, the Prince wondered if he would recognize the Sorcerer after so many years.

Antique and vine-covered were the walls of the modest cottage at the pathway's end. Several smaller outbuildings, a few attached to the main structure and some freestanding nearby, seemed of equally ancient vintage. The structures stood in a wide clearing near the center of the shallow valley, and behind the clearing a pine woods climbed the far hills and disappeared over the top on the other side.

"This is quite strange," the Prince observed to his closest attendant when no one came out to greet the visitors. He dismounted. A peculiar scent pervading the air near the cottage seemed familiar, yet the Prince could not quite place it. It seemed to create an inexplicable uneasiness among the already nervous party. The horses rolled their eyes, flattened their ears against bobbing heads, and grew almost impossible to control.

The mysterious character of the Sorcerer had long tickled the wings of the Prince's imagination, so now the anticipation of meeting him face to face jousted with, then quickly overcame his fears. He strode boldly up to the front door and raised his fist to knock.

Unexpectedly the door jerked open, and the Prince almost lost his balance. Before him stood a hoary, cloak-wrapped, yet strangely majestic gentleman. Framed in the rustic doorway, his hair and beard were silver-gray, and his eyes burned in his head like spiral galaxies set into deep wrinkles of the morning sky. "I am the Sorcerer," he said.

The Prince took an involuntary step backward.

"I have been waiting for you," the Sorcerer continued, looking directly at the Prince and ignoring the rest of the royal retinue. "Come in, please. Alone."

The Prince motioned for his attendants to stay where they were and stepped through the doorway. The Sorcerer led him into the kitchen and to a low doorway against the opposite wall. He had to duck to pass through. Inside the next room the ceiling was too low for them to stand upright except toward the middle of the room. The Sorcerer closed the door behind them.

The chamber was windowless and lit by an oil lamp hanging from the high beam in the center. All around the Prince were bottles, vials, bins, and glass containers of every description, all labeled in a strange, unrecognizable script. Along two walls of the room ancient books filled shelves which extended into the darkness beyond the lamp's circle of light, and several books lay open and marked upon a table below the lamp. Dust was everywhere, even upon the pages of the open books, as if they had long been neglected. The Prince had the distinct feeling that someone else was in the room with them, but when he glanced around into the dark corners and shadowy recesses where the fingers of lamplight could not quite reach, he could discern no other human shape in the darkness.

The Prince took the King's sealed message from inside his shirt and offered it to the Sorcerer. The wizard accepted it, but laid it down unopened on the dusty table.

"What may I do for you?" the Sorcerer asked with an ironic smile that told the Prince he already knew.

"I have been suffering a grave discontent," the Prince began more boldly than he felt. "The discomfort is sometimes so terrible that I feel a physical pain, here, like a knot in my stomach. I can find no relief for my depression, nor solutions to my puzzlement. I am craving to know with certainty whether life has a purpose, and just where I might fit into it all. I need to know why there is anything at all, and not rather nothing."

The Prince paused in the hope that his interlocutor might offer him a simple answer, but the Sorcerer remained silent. In the silence the Prince thought he perceived a faint breathing from the darkness just behind him.

"The King, my father," the Prince continued, "decided to send me to you for some sort of purgative. The University and the Church have done me no good whatsoever, and I believe the King now fears that I am possessed by evil spirits. He seeks your help in ridding me of these endless questions about purpose, meaning, and understanding of the true nature of things." He paused again, and then in a lower voice, as if someone might be listening, confided, "But in truth, I have come in the hope that you might be able to help me find the answers to my questions."

"I see," was all the Sorcerer said. He turned to a narrow workbench in the dim light near one of the low eaves, measured some materials from several drawers of a wooden apothecary chest into the porcelain bowl of a large mortar, ground and mixed adroitly with a wooden pestle, and poured the contents of the vessel into a small leather pouch he took from a low cabinet. He handed the pouch to the Prince.

"What's this?"

"Mushrooms," replied the Sorcerer. "Mostly mushrooms. With a pinch of ergot, some ground-up mandrake root, and a few other odds and ends. But mostly mushrooms."

"But why . . . how can this help me? I thought perhaps you might allow me to stay for a while . . . study with you . . . "

"You said you have an irresistible craving for certainty. Perhaps these can be of some help. Take about half at a time, but no more. I have given you enough for two doses."

The Prince looked carefully at the strange old pouch. Intricately tooled on one side was a crescent moon and some characters he did not recognize. "When should I take them?"

"Watch for the right time," the Sorcerer replied. "Quietly. Attentively. Like the frog waits for an insect."

"Like a frog?"

"Yes. You'll feel when it is appropriate. Come back if you still have questions." He opened the low door and led the way back through the kitchen, held the door for the Prince, and they both stepped outside.

The attendants and bodyguards were obviously relieved that their charge had reappeared. Two attendants quickly brought the Prince his skittish stallion as he and the wizard shook hands and exchanged farewells. All made ready to depart. But before mounting, the Prince paused in thought, and then walked back to the Sorcerer, who still stood in the doorway to the kitchen. Indicating the pouch of mushrooms, the Prince inquired in a low voice, "Is this intended to give me answers, as I want, or to purge me of the questions, as the King wants?"

"Is there a difference?" smiled the Sorcerer.

The Prince's eye was suddenly caught by a movement in the kitchen behind the wizard. In the flash of an instant the Prince clearly saw the form of a woman disappear through the low doorway into the dusty room where he and the magician had just talked. Though brief, the impact of the glimpse was powerful, for the vision was of the most beautiful woman the Prince had ever seen. Before that obscure passageway swallowed her back into its darkness, he beheld her as if in a crystalline blaze that was more than reality. Her face was white and perfect, framed by long raven tresses that cascaded down her supple shoulders and back, her eyes flashed green, and the graceful movement of her slender figure was quietly feline. Her image consumed him like a vibration so perfectly tuned to his soul that it smote a mighty responsive chord within him whose every note was precisely in place, perfectly blended, and irresistible.

She apparently had been watching them, and when the Prince had noticed her, she withdrew without a word. The Sorcerer did not turn around. Amused, curious, he studied the Prince's reaction.

Dumbfounded, the Prince opened his mouth to speak. The Sorcerer just shook his head. "If you have more questions, we will talk another time."

The Prince did not move, but peered insistently past the Sorcerer to the doorway on the opposite wall of the kitchen, and he leaned slightly forward, as if to better see through the wall itself and into the darkness.

"Later," commanded the Sorcerer, firmly blocking the Prince's way. "After you have allowed the medicine a chance to do its work." The interview was clearly at an end.

By an act of sheer will the Prince regained control of himself. As if waking from a dream, he bid the Sorcerer farewell once again, returned to his chestnut stallion, still restrained by the two patient attendants, and mounted. The royal cavalcade formed in order for the return, but just before signaling the departure, the Prince broke from the formation and rode over to the doorway where the Sorcerer still stood impassively.

The Prince secretly touched the leather pouch safe within his robes and asked, "Should I watch for anything in particular?"

The Sorcerer knew well how treacherous weather conditions could be on the mountain at this time of year, particularly with the royal party getting such a late start. "Watch for the fog," he advised, amid the clatter of hooves, for just at that moment a gust of wind whipped up a small dust devil and the Prince's horse shied abruptly away.

"The 'frog'?" asked the Prince, through the dust and commotion, spinning around to regain control of his steed.

"Yes," called the Sorcerer, not really hearing clearly. "So that you may have a safe trip."

"Very well," responded the Prince, puzzled, and he returned to his place at the head of the cavalcade. He gazed over his shoulder past the cloaked form standing in the doorway, into the still kitchen he guarded. The royal party rode off with the Prince still looking back, until they topped the crest of the first hill and started the steep descent down the mountainside.

The Prince had much time to think during the long ride back to the castle. *What will the mushrooms show me*, he wondered. *And what will be the significance of a frog that I am to watch for? How will it guide me through a safe trip?* But most of all he thought of the beautiful black-haired woman whom he had glimpsed and who now would not vacate the premises of his most secret thoughts. Nor, it should be added, had the Prince any inclination to give her notice to terminate the mental tenancy. *Somehow they must all be linked together*, he thought, *though I cannot yet figure out just how: the mushrooms, the frog, the dark-haired woman.* His thoughts swam dizzily and he could not solve the elusive riddles, try though he might.

CHAPTER SEVEN

The Prince Discovers the Animal

The King had already spent a busy week interviewing candidates for the newly vacated post of Chief Advisor. Applicants had arrived from the farthest corners of the realm, and the King seemed to be making no headway in the task. Some of his close retainers suggested to one another that he was being scrupulously cautious in selecting precisely the right man to fill the important office, competently replace Grimm, and achieve the proper harmony with the King's own personal political leanings, petty idiosyncrasies, and subtle sovereign fetishes. Others were quick to point out that the King was probably incapable of making such a weighty decision without the advice of a Chief Advisor, and thus the office would never again be filled.

Grimm himself seemed not the least perturbed by his abrupt dismissal from office and consequential loss of rank. He enjoyed wandering the balmy castle grounds without further responsibility, babbling happily to himself, as free and unmolested as a ghost of the forgotten dead. He knew perfectly well things were unfolding as they ought. Hadn't God himself said so?

The Prince, when he returned, decided it was best not to bother the busy King. Instead, he waited for a sign that the time was ripe to consume the medicinal mushrooms vouchsafed to him by the Sorcerer. But he was not sure just what he was watching for, or if he would recognize it when it came.

One morning the Prince awoke in a cold sweat. Frightened. Agitated. Out of breath. He had dreamt that a giant spotted frog pinned a lovely raven-haired maiden against the top of an enormous mushroom cap. She writhed and screamed for help, and to the dreaming Prince the calamity was both frightening and erotic. Though he tried with all his might to reach and rescue her, his feet slipped on the viscous incline of the mushroom cap and he could not close the distance to her. The smirking frog reached out with malevolent, stubby arms and hideous scaly claws to slowly pry apart her creamy thighs as the Prince watched in helpless horror and increasing sexual excitement. Then he awoke.

The Prince looked around his own room, safe within the heart of the royal castle. He shook his head to break free the residual debris of frustration. A foul taste had painted the four walls of his mouth. He picked up the pouch of mushrooms which nightly he had been placing with great ceremony on the small stand beside his bed and wondered if today was the day to ingest the portion. That very morning he had planned an informal croquet practice, and he could easily make arrangements to tour the royal playing green alone. The weather looked clear. Perhaps the dream was the very sign he had been waiting for.

"Why not?" the Prince inquired of the empty chamber. He climbed gingerly out of bed and carefully poured the contents of the pouch onto the top of a small marble table, measured out two unequal piles, and scraped the larger one back into the pouch. He was able to recognize the mushroom parts as he poked through the dry gray powder: a fragment of a cap, a piece of stem, broken annulus and gills. He ate the measured portion. "Not bad," he said to himself. "Dry, but palatable." He licked his fingers and drew the tie on the pouch, saving the rest for later.

The Prince dressed quickly and headed for the croquet green. Politely he instructed the greens keeper to exclude his usual companions from the field today, making it quite clear that he did not want to be disturbed that morning. He then dismissed his attendants, offering no explanation. A crown prince is not expected to offer explanations, after all.

He undertook his usual morning round of croquet, selecting the red ball, as was his custom, and of course the red-ringed mallet. He sniffed at the breeze. The morning sun felt good. *He* felt good, by golly. Quap! Out through the first two wickets shot the glimmering red ball into splendid playing position. He worked his way carefully around the eastern side of the course.

When he had reached the stake half-way around the green, the Prince paused to gaze at his own shadow, which had grown curiously animated and independent. He glanced slowly around the course and wondered if the mushrooms were producing any noticeable effect on his perception. No sooner did he turn his attention thus inward, however, than things began to take on an unsettlingly reptilian cast. The more he paid heed to the feeling, the more it seemed to be swallowing him like a large snake. He decided it would be best to play on.

As the young Prince turned this way and that, trying to remember precisely what pattern he was supposed to be following in accordance with the royal rules, lurking things rose up out of the corners of his eye. He knocked the strangely shimmering red spheroid through scaly terrors, which brandished long greenish teeth and quivering claws. He most certainly did not enjoy the way they had begun to conceal themselves in the patches of wavering lawn and then spring up horribly just where he was about to set his foot. The reptiles gave him some uncomfortable moments without doubt, but the Prince knew them to be fundamentally the figments they were. A hard, critical stare and a modicum of self-possession would reduce a lurking horror into a mere shadow and yawning jaws into an irregularity in the grass. He held the monstrous at bay with the power of human reason, and with no little pride. "Is this all the Sorcerer can show me?" he bragged out loud.

As he proceeded through the back wickets and started home, however, he became increasingly unnerved by the growing suspicion, which swelled to a palpable certainty, that he was becoming one of *them*. He mucked about in the swampy ooze of disbelief, an alligator tail, ridged backbone, scales, snake eyes that blinked sideways, and razor-sharp lizard claws that gripped and flailed an increasingly meaningless mallet. His blood ran cold. He tried to blink these visions out of existence and his mind back into a more human perspective, but what force was there in the blink of a gold-slitted frog eye? His reason undermined, he could no longer concentrate on the tenuous web-fabric of a human world because of his overwhelming desire to sun himself on a warm rock.

Time passed with quiet, reptilian certitude, and the Prince was oblivious to its passage. He awoke as if from a living dream and found himself sitting comfortably beside a small, dead lilac bush at the edge of the croquet field, warm and content in the afternoon sun. He saw neither ball nor mallet, and neither seemed important enough for him to get up and look for. No, he was much more interested in what he was feeling. He seemed somehow separate from himself. With the reptiles, he had been both frightened and unafraid, all at the same time. Instinctively he wanted to recoil in horror, but an isolated part of himself knew there was nothing to fear, it was all just his own imagination. Now he saw and felt himself as an animal warming itself in the tall grass, and the animal felt good. Yet he was separate from the animal that he was.

The Prince stood up, or rather, the Prince willed his animal to stand up and was amused and amazed that it was able to do so quite competently. "It walks," he whispered in awe as he ambled slowly away from the croquet field. "It breathes in me. It beats my heart."

And while his mind was occupied with these and other curious observations, the Prince turned over the task of walking entirely to the animal. His mind, free from the responsibility of operating the animal, could now soar over more lofty landscapes. His thoughts wandered, and so did his animal, though each through a different terrain.

A long, curving flagstone walkway followed the contour of the hillside and linked the croquet field with the royal castle. On the uphill side, to the Prince's right as he strolled, were the tall, stately pines of the Imperial Forest, and the air was rich with their poignant piney scent. To his left, distant fields opened like a giant passion flower in the afternoon sun. He walked without effort, and his arms and legs felt full of limitless energy, buoyancy, and animal joy.

The Prince wanted to gaze out at the distant horizon, but found that his animal was monopolizing the use of his eyes to measure its steps across the irregular flagstone path. He reined himself to a stop for a moment to borrow back his eyesight, and the distant hills invited him like the soft virgin-down-covered flanks of a supine earth mother. Distant cattle grazed like miniature replicas of toy cows. He let a burble of joy squirm up through his teeth, then, relinquishing the use of his eyes once again to his animal, continued on along the path. He rode majestically atop his animal, looking out through its eyes.

The Prince had been walking the homeward path for as long as he could remember when it occurred to him that he had actually not gone very far, only about a quarter of the way back. "How curious," he murmured. "Time is running so exquisitely slow." But then it seemed to him that time was not running at all, but was disjointed like a line of ducks parading through a shooting gallery. He wondered what it would be like to be a few steps ahead of himself, and when he got there, he found it to be the total present. He wondered what it would be like to be at all the places he had been, was, and would be along that footpath at precisely the same time. What would it feel like to be a continuous stream of walkers, of walking, along the entire length of the path all at once? "That, surely, would be to perceive eternity," his mind said to him absently, as if addressing someone else. And then in his imagination he *was* at all those places all at once. He felt the physical and temporal extension as palpably as peanut butter spread upon dry toast. For an instant he seemed to have burrowed like a worm into the very heart of being, and then with the almost audible flutter of a deck of cards dropping onto a sheet of taut canvas, the instant collapsed back in upon itself and the Prince was again at a single time and place.

As he rounded a bend in the path, the Prince came upon Grimm, the King's exiled Chief Advisor, sitting with his aged legs crossed before him and his back pressed rigidly against the gnarled trunk of an old sycamore tree. He appeared to be asleep, or possibly even dead, so the Prince approached him with great caution. When he was just a few feet away, he squatted down, bringing his eyes level with those of the old man.

Grimm was gazing implacably back at him through narrow slits of nearly closed eyelids. His eyes seemed to flash with the old lightning of a bygone era. The Prince sat down, fascinated. As the Prince stared in wonder, wrinkles seemed to be swimming across Grimm's face like a moving sea, breaking in living waves upon the beachheads of his eyes, ears, and mouth. The pure burning whiteness

of his hair and eyebrows sizzled as it was quenched in the calm pool
of the Prince's mind. An almost imperceptible, ironic smile turned up
the corners of the ancient lips.

For the first time in his life, and without a word being spoken,
the Prince felt he understood Grimm perfectly, implicitly, overwhelm-
ingly. He could feel what it was like to be the old man. With deep
reverence and compassion the Prince calmly comprehended the
predicament: Grimm's animal had grown old and was now failing
him. The Prince's eyes grew moist, and in that moment it seemed as
if Grimm knew that the Prince understood.

The hoary head nodded slightly, and Grimm asked, "What may
I do for you, my lord?"

The Prince was taken aback and suddenly uncertain whether
he was capable of speaking. He cleared his throat. Then as if from a
great distance he heard his own voice asking, "Can you advise me on
a matter of some importance?"

"Of course." Grimm's voice was a deep rumble.

Almost without willing it, the Prince asked one of the
questions that had been gnawing like a rat at a corner of his mind ever
since he had left the Sorcerer: "What guidance might I expect from a
frog?"

"A frog? Did you say, '*a frog*'?"

The Prince nodded.

Grimm tipped his head slightly to the side and his eyes stared
vacantly, as if he were listening to some distant sounds the Prince
could not hear. In a few moments the venerable head straightened and
the eyes were watching him once again. "Frogs are composite things,"
the ex-Chief Advisor began slowly, as if explaining a difficult concept
to a child. "And as such, they are subject to decay. I must advise you
not to waste too much time on frogs."

As far as the Prince was concerned, Grimm had just encapsu-
lated the utter truth within a few brittle, dancing words. There was
nothing left to be said. He struggled to regain his feet, bowed deeply,
and without another word turned away to follow the flagstone path
back to the castle.

At the castle the Prince watched and listened and felt the

wonder inherent in the most ordinary acts and objects. He studied the perfect way the hairs grew out of the ear of an old attendant and wept at the exquisite simplicity of the hourly chimes. Every instant seemed full to the brim with miracles of the most subtle and profound nature, and he and his animal were an integral part of it all.

Later, at dinnertime, the elderly servant who seated him asked the Prince if he was hungry.

"Golly! I honestly don't know," the Prince tittered. "Why don't you just set that bowl of vichyssoise in front of my animal and we'll see if it eats, okay?"

The poor servant, of course, did not understand, and in his distress forgot to warm the water in the royal finger bowls, much to the displeasure of the King. The Prince, on the other hand, felt more at peace and at home in the universe than he could ever remember feeling.

The Prince ate with unbridled gusto, scraping his plate with a crust of bread and lifting his bowl like a peasant to drain off the last dregs. Afterwards he felt full and content as a flatulent cat. His head nodded and he yawned. "I think I'll put my animal to bed now," he was heard to say to no one in particular as he left the dining room. "I think it's ready to sleep."

CHAPTER EIGHT

The Animal Consumes the Prince

Well, my son," beamed the King as robustly as the sunshine streaming through the open windows, "and has our good friend the Sorcerer given you a little something for your indisposition?"

"Yes, father." The Prince had happened upon the King's procession unexpectedly in the wide corridor which led from the castle's main entrance to the throne room. Since he had taken the wizard's prescription nearly a week before, the feeling of intermeshed reality and illusion had abated only incrementally day by day. His mind still wandered, and his return to the royal reality was not yet complete. He had been avoiding his father and felt disinclined to discuss the matter with him.

"Are you cured then?" his father boomed, swatting the Prince encouragingly across the shoulders.

"I've only taken half the remedy as yet, father. I shall know its full value only when the entire regimen has run its course."

"Very well, my boy. You come tell me all about it when you're finished." He put his arm around his son's shoulders and walked him a few steps along the bright corridor at the head of a long train of attendants. "You know, I have every confidence in the Sorcerer. He's been a good friend of mine for these many years, though I haven't had the pleasure of visiting with him personally for quite some time. Pressures of running the kingdom, you know."

The Prince bowed, and the King and his royal retinue marched onward toward the throne room to continue the exhaustive first round of interviews for the replacement of the Chief Advisor. The attendants were all costumed alike in shiny black-and-yellow striped togs with gossamer capes that made them look to the Prince like a solemn procession of fat, wet bumble bees parading after their queen.

The Prince sighed and sat down on the marble stairway which led to the royal counting house above. Had the Sorcerer's medicine done him any good, he wondered. *Indeed*, he thought, *I have discovered the animal. But what good is that, really? The animal has its place in the universe, no doubt, but I am as much at sea as ever. If the Sorcerer's drugs were intended to give me a vision of where I fit into all this that is reality, I surely cannot see it. And if it was intended to still my questioning, then it has been a dismal failure.*

The Prince's thoughts returned to the black-haired woman he recalled only vaguely now. He was alone, so he took the pouch from inside his shirt where it hung from a leather cord, pulled open the draw string, and pondered its contents. All he had was the mushrooms. He had seen no frogs, and the mysterious woman was only a distant memory. Impulsively he began to eat the remaining contents of the little pouch.

"My goodness!" he exclaimed when he saw what he was doing, or rather, what his animal was doing, for the action was certainly without his reasoned approval. "I wonder how this will go with shuttleball?" he whispered apprehensively. It was already early afternoon and almost time for the Imperial Shuttleball Practice. "Oh, what the hell." He turned the empty pouch inside out and licked the last of the fine powder that clung to the rough leather. "The animal did it, so the animal can suffer the consequences."

Shuttleball was taken very seriously at the castle, as were most sports. The Prince found himself somehow more fleet of foot and light of hand than usual that particular day, and his legs and arms seemed to posses an infinite reserve of energy. He stationed himself between baselines on the inbound net, shuttlebat lashed tightly to his forearm, and waited raptly for the opposing team to serve. When the ball veered his way, he dove, dug, shuttled, swung, and spiked with a joyful intensity he had never felt before. Once or twice he inquired of himself if he was feeling anything from the mushrooms, but the question seemed unimportant and a distraction from the game at hand, so he forced it out of his mind. He dwelt not on form or style, but responded purely to the bobbing movement of the ball as it shuttled back and forth across the nets. The game absorbed him totally.

His team won a close victory, and he felt splendid to be a part of the intricate team effort. Heartily he congratulated his teammates, then retired to the royal locker room.

There, among the birchwood lockers, fear gripped his insides with a slippery hand. Vainly he fought to collect his thoughts. Not that things actually *looked* different, right to left, top to bottom, back to front. No, but their *significance* was somehow different. Far or near, long or short, high or low, animate or inanimate all had a different *meaning*. The shuttleball at his feet was twice as large as a croquet ball, but if he stared at it in a certain way, it became enormous enough to swallow the entire universe in an insidiously brown-stitched manner.

The narrow walkway between the lockers to the shower room seemed to stretch out to an infinite length when he began to traverse it, though he could clearly see the gray tile of the shower room floor just ahead. And when he paused for a moment to reflect, the wooden doors beside him began to swell and contract with his breathing, though nothing actually moved.

"Thank God this didn't hit me when I was on the shuttleball court," he whispered. "I wouldn't have been able to play!"

He managed somehow to soap, rinse, and dry himself, but only with great difficulty. Clothed again, he escaped through a back door of the building and fled to the stables. He grunted terse instructions to the stable hand, and his hands seemed to wave about wildly like frantic birds impaled on the stumps of his arms. While he waited for his horse to be saddled, he clung firmly to a rough post of the corral fence, praying he would not explode into some unimaginable and unprincely behavior or collapse babbling and puking into the dust. Bright sun, dusty boots, for a dizzying eternity he was able to restrain himself.

Mounted at last and riding away by himself, the Prince began to feel much better. "Trust the animal," he said to himself over and over again. He perceived the absurdity of the situation: he rode atop his animal even as they both rode atop this chestnut stallion he knew so well. In darkness on a familiar trail, he thought to himself, it is best for the horseman to loosen the reins and allow the animal to find its own footing. In a flash he saw clearly that relinquishing the reins was precisely what he had been doing at the shuttleball game! He had not interfered with his animal as it played the game, had not queried, "Ought I this?" or "Dare I that?" or "Am I able?" or even "How do I feel?" Uninhibited by such meaningless inquiry, the animal was able to involve itself completely in the development of the game, and with good success. The mind, thought the Prince, only interferes with the animal's natural activity. The mind holds the animal back.

The Prince trotted along contentedly, allowing his animal free rein to control the reins of the larger animal upon which they both rode. His mind wandered. The past was forgotten, and his direction was aimless. He beheld the different greens of the forest and fields, was astonished by the regularity of each maple leaf, felt the warm breeze upon his cheeks and against the tiny hairs on the backs of his hands, and savored the dank, horsey smell of his stallion. Each moment was an ever-new and unique experience. His animal kept the stallion at the proper pace. "Perhaps better than I could do myself," he muttered.

At the old mill he dismounted and tied up the horse. The Prince knew of a pleasant meadow just across the millstream and up a small, sparsely wooded hillside. It would be splendid to lie there in the afternoon sun. As he strolled down the path towards the crossing where the millrace began, he made a mental note to take over control of his animal when he got to the stream. The crossing was treacherous at this time of year, requiring careful attention to the selection of a proper route across various stepping stones and fallen logs. His animal could be trusted to ride a horse or walk down the trail while his mind played with the wind in the trees and the nature of reality, but when a serious judgment decision presented itself, then he would surely have to take control himself. He would weigh the complex parameters and undertake the best-reasoned course of action.

The woods were lovely, and the music of the stream and the gurgling of the millrace were seductive sirens. How beautiful it was just to be alive and breathing the cool, woodsy air! The Prince wandered through the back roads of his mind. *The present is not very broad*, he was thinking as he stepped out onto the first of a series of slippery rocks, not noticing that he had undertaken the tricky crossing absentmindedly. *Indeed, the patterns of water surrounding these rocks are shorter than the shortest sentence, narrower than a state-of-being verb*, he thought to himself as he leaped from stone to log to stone again, solving the maze unconsciously, picking the perfect path without picking at all.

"Gracious!" the Prince exclaimed a few feet from the opposite bank, suddenly realizing what he was doing. He tottered precariously astride a wet stone and in a panic took one long, springing leap toward the far bank. The gap was too great and the Prince splashed and splattered, sputtering up onto the dry ground, wet to his knees. He sat down to empty the water from his shoes.

"My animal didn't even summon me back for the crossing!"

A blinding white light shone in the Prince's eyes. On another, more ordinary day, he might have described it simply as a pencil of sunlight piercing the shadowy trunks of the woods. But today it seemed as if great peace and absolute certainty blazed upon him and ignited his soul, reflecting in the mill creek and illuminating everything around him with an ethereal dancing sparkle. He suddenly comprehended beyond doubt that he was not more than his animal. In one magic, ludicrous, uproarious instant he saw clearly that all he was, *was* the animal. The Prince roared with laughter at the cosmic joke that he had thought "he" sat somewhere up in the corner judging the "animal". The "animal" had undertaken to cross the stream, a task "he" had planned to reserve for "his" personal domain of higher brain functions, of judgment, of ultimate control. And the "animal" would have successfully crossed the stream had "he" not panicked and leapt for shore. But even the "he" that took the leap, he now saw lucidly, *was* the animal, responding through a slightly more convoluted series of neural pathways, waltzing hypnotically to a tune piped by the exigencies of the environment. All the fears, the judgments, the conversations, internal and external, the laughter--*all was the animal*, locked into a closed loop of harmonic reactions to the habitat like an organ stop played by the relentless fingers of the cosmic organist. "Even the 'I' that sits back in the corner of my mind and watches the animal, that judges it good or bad, *is* the animal, too," he roared. "There is nothing left over to call 'me'!"

When his laughter had subsided, the Prince found himself engulfed in a powerful feeling of well-being. More than ever before in his life, he felt totally at home in the world, just as it was. Everything was exquisitely beautiful and fit together just so. The Suchness of it all brought tears of joy to his eyes. Bound up with the well-being, the familiarity, and the perfect Suchness, as all colors are bound up in the spectrum of white light, he felt a concomitant wave of great sorrow for all creatures, including himself, who suffered the blistering need to prove their own worthiness. Slowly he stood up. *The animal imagines itself to be more than it is*, he pondered sadly and began to stroll along the bank. *It dreams it is me.*

A small green frog hopped from his path with a "squeak" and splished into the cold stream.

"The frog!" The Prince smiled. "You are to show me a safe journey." He bowed in appreciation of the apparent far-reaching wisdom of the Sorcerer.

"Squeak"– splish! "Squeak"– splish! Frogs cleared the royal pathway like miniature green paratroopers. "Squeak, squeak"– splish! splish! The path seemed to lead him ever deeper into the heart of true understanding.

As he walked on, the Prince began to perceive that everything was going on at the same time, the beating of his heart, his breathing, the weaving thoughts, the hopping, squeaking, splishing frogs, the flowing stream, the rustling of the trees, the piercing cry of a startled jay, the faraway barking of two dogs, the Sorcerer's watchfulness from the mountain top, the spinning, wobbling, revolving of the earth, the steady ticking of the vast clockwork universe--all infinitely interrelated, interpenetrating, and all present at the same instant, all at once, only to pass away completely in the next instant, absolutely to make room for a spanking new creation, an entirely different present, thin as a knife blade. A series of discrete instants presented themselves in no necessary order. It made him joyful and sad at the same time. "And I will die away too," he said to the trunks of the transient pines. "And leave no trace."

The Prince's perfect contentment, however, could not hold back its own demise. Soon the light began to fade, and wet legs and the oncoming evening chill sent a shiver deep into his bones. He waded back across the millstream and found his horse, anxious for its evening oats, just as the last of the daylight evaporated like steam from the cooling forest. He mounted, and as he rode back toward the castle, the Prince glanced over his shoulder to try to catch one last glimpse of the island of contentment that had long since passed by. There was, of course, nothing left to be seen.

CHAPTER NINE

The Fall From Grace

It has been said by men who are considered wise, "Woe be to him who has grasped the perfect moment, for the rest of his days shall suffer by comparison." So the Prince recalled portions of the insights that had so deeply touched him by the millstream, but he could not recapture the feeling of certitude and perfect fulfillment that had washed over him like a storm tide and then had withdrawn forever from the deserted beach of his emotional equilibrium. It was as if God had spoken the truth to him in a dream on the condition that he would not quite remember it upon awakening. As if he might never again achieve cerebral orgasm.

Where he had been listless before, he now grew downright irritable. For long hours he wandered alone through the Imperial Forest or else down beside the millstream, perhaps in the hope of attaining once again the communion with the essential he had so poignantly experienced there, perhaps only to escape for the time being from the petty prattlings and inane posturings of the castle's pomp and ceremony or the empty exertions upon the fields of sport.

To the amazement of the entire castle population, and not the least the Prince himself, he began to take pleasure in spending time with Grimm, conversing quietly beneath a banyan tree or strolling slowly about the imperial grounds. He was unable to determine if this was so because the relinquishment of responsibility had allowed lucidity to return to the antique advisor, or whether the consumption of mushrooms had so fundamentally deranged the Prince's own perceptions that advanced senile dementia now took on the ring of clarity and incisiveness. It was altogether possible that he and Grimm now shared delusions in conflict with consensus reality.

As Grimm grew to trust the young Heir Apparent, he began to

relate fragments of his dialogues with God. The Prince would listen patiently, neither judging nor criticizing the older man's confidences. The recurring theme underlying the divine revelations was the Lord's increasing displeasure with the way man was trashing up His creation by fleshly wickedness and evil. The Almighty was on the verge of calling off the whole business, of wiping man and fish and bird and beast from the face of His otherwise pristine planet. "He's mad as hell, and I think He's about to do it," Grimm would moan.

"I wouldn't worry about it too much," the Prince soothed. "It's completely out of our control." His experience at the Church of Nod had dampened his theological appetite, and the mushrooms had precipitated a temper of amused fatalism.

One day the King sent a message to his son "inviting" him to preside at the Annual Water Lily Festival the following month in the ancient town of Enosville. The Prince declined, offering no excuse other than that he really did not feel up to it. Exasperated by the offhanded dismissal of his veiled command, the King quickly issued an imperial summons for the Prince to attend at once an audience in the throne room. The Prince might have ignored that too had his father not taken the precaution of charging his beefy reeve with collaring the young Heir Apparent and escorting him personally into the royal presence.

The King was still out of sorts over his chronic inability to fill the vacant Chief Advisor post. The Prime Manicurist had almost finished the fingernails of the royal left hand when the Prince was summarily ushered into the grand throne room.

"You wish to see me father?" The Prince knelt in the prescribed manner, but with a demonstrable lack of enthusiasm.

"Yes, yes indeed!" the King bellowed, waving his right hand wildly about in a combination of gestures designed to add regal punctuation and at the same time facilitate the drying of his nails. "What's this I hear about your abandoning the poor Enosvillers and their lovely water lilies? You presided there last year, did you not?"

"Yes, father."

"Well, we mustn't let them think they're being slighted, now, must we?" The King's voice dripped with rhetorical unction.

The Prince did not attempt an answer.

"Come here, my son." The King indicated the empty Chief Advisor's chair. "Sit down and let's have a little chat." When the Prince was seated at the King's side, the sovereign continued in a more fatherly, but no less histrionic tone. "And have you found answers to your burning questions, my son?"

"I look for no further answers just now, father."

The manicurist finished the left hand, which the King now waved ceremoniously about. "And what have you found, my dear boy? Come, come, you must tell me."

"The purgative was effective," the Prince responded evasively. "I no longer seek answers which I do not already have."

The King suspected dimly that he was being put off, so he abandoned the fatherly tact. He pondered as deeply as he was able. "Are you ill?"

"No, father."

"Have you any reason at all why you should disdain the adoration and devotion of our subjects at the Water Lily Festival?"

"Only that the prospect of the festival does not amuse me."

The King raised his eyebrows incredulously. "Doesn't *amuse* you! Doesn't amuse *you*!"

"No, father."

"Well it damn well amuses *me*! Enosville supports the crown solidly, both politically and financially, and by God it deserves a royal personage at its asinine Water Lily Festival. *I* certainly don't have the time to be running over there for such nonsense."

"Let someone who cares about it preside," the Prince offered apathetically.

The King glowered at the Prince, searching for just the right words, which as usual were slow in coming. A frowning, speechless regent can be a frightening sight indeed, but the Prince seemed unperturbed, as if the King's silly concerns were no longer his. Indifference waved like a red flag before the King's bull mood. He jerked around and swatted the Prince soundly on the shoulder, half to vent his spleen, and half to capture the young man's wandering attention. "What in God's name has happened to you!" he shouted.

The Prince, nearly knocked off the chair by the unexpected blow, raised his arms in defense, but when he saw that the attack was over, lapsed again into his previous torpor.

"I'm told you've all but given up sports," the King raged. "Now you refuse to take part in your royal functions. Your attendants have reported to us that you spend your time smelling wild flowers, chasing moonbeams through the woods, or lollygagging with that batty old fart I just threw out of my court. What's gotten into you? I'm not just talking about sleeping late every now and then, or missing an occasional shuttleball practice, or even refusing to preside at this God-forsaken Water Lily Festival. But a king has got to be a king, and a prince, a prince. It's the principle of the matter! What could you possibly be *thinking*?" The King peered intently at his son as if he actually expected an answer this time.

The Prince cleared his throat, then began slowly, "I've just been looking at things a little differently of late, father. Everything seems to be fixed and beyond our control. You know? Like chips in the irresistible flow of a mighty river. Why struggle? Peace is found within anyway, is it not?"

The King's mouth dropped open in disbelief. He had never heard the Prince, nor *anyone*, for that matter, prattle on in just such a post-hallucinogenic manner.

"What's the use," continued the Prince, hardly noticing the King's reaction. "I've taken the Sorcerer's medicine. I've caught a brief glimpse of the truth. We're all in it together, whether we like it or not. It's as intricate as a butterfly's wing, as irrefutable as a granite cliff, and as overwhelming as the star-studded sky on a moonless night. How do I even know anything actually exists outside my own mind, after all?"

This was too much for the King. Leaping to his feet, he yanked the Prince up by the collar and shook him violently. "Try this on for reality!" he bellowed, and pitched him rudely back into the chair. The beet-red monarch loomed over his son, huffing and fuming. "What has the Sorcerer done to you? Just what drugs has he given you, anyway?"

"Why, just a mild purgative, my–"

"'Purgative' indeed," the King stormed. "It seems to have purged your reason! The Sorcerer has brainwashed the Crown Prince of Nod. This smacks of high treason most foul!"

"Perhaps if I could talk to him--"

"Silence! You've said quite enough already. The Sorcerer shall answer to *us*, if any more talking is to be done!" The King marshaled his overtaxed wits. He turned to an attendant cowering nearby. "Bring the Sorcerer to us at once! Take this message to him: the King bids you come to the castle forthwith to explain the condition of the Prince."

The Prince tried to intercede, but the King silenced him again with a menacing wave of his jeweled scepter. He made the trembling attendant repeat the message twice, and without further ceremony dispatched him on his way. The King scowled at his son, then stormed out of the throne room.

As the sobering days which followed this volatile encounter crept slowly past, the King's righteous wrath subsided, and the regal heart softened. Each day seemed to bring the Prince back a little more from his reverie, back into the royal reality of the King's court. On the third day, the Prince even ventured once again onto the shuttleball court, though the King's men reported that he seemed less than totally absorbed in the contest.

On the fourth day, Grimm learned that the Sorcerer had been angrily summoned, and he was severely agitated and distraught. He hastily made his way to the grand throne room to seek a special audience with the King, which was promptly granted. The old man's hands shook and he looked older and more decrepit than the King remembered, but a light of conviction burned in his eyes and the power of dread quickened his voice. "You shouldn't have done it, your majesty. I know who the Sorcerer really *is*, and He's already mad as hell and can destroy us all with the twitch of a finger."

The King had grown increasingly apprehensive about his impending confrontation with the wizard, so this news, even from the feebleminded, was less than heartening. He drew a deep breath. "What can I do? Perhaps the Sorcerer will ignore my summons, as he has always done in the past." It seemed to everyone who heard him that he hoped it would be so.

On the fifth day, the King and the Prince met again in the grand throne room and conversed at length. The unpleasantness of the earlier encounter had vanished completely. The Prince agreed to preside at the Water Lily Festival as long as he could travel to and from Enosville all in the same day. This was not only agreeable to the King, but considering his own recollections of the loathsome accommodations in Enosville, seemed to be sound good sense. He was immensely pleased and congratulated everyone on his son's speedy recovery.

On the morning of the sixth day the King's messenger returned with the magician's reply. The Sorcerer would arrive early the next morning.

CHAPTER TEN

The King Confronts Sorcery

The Imperial Throne room was still, but no calm inhabited the hearts of the King and his courtiers. The Chief Advisor's chair loomed uncomfortably empty at the King's right elbow. He had sent an invitation to Grimm to sit in on the interview with the Sorcerer, but the old man was nowhere to be found.

The elegant velvet curtains that covered the lofty walls menaced, as if they concealed archers. One of the hidden archers near the door let out a muffled sneeze. *"Gesundheit!"* responded the drapes behind the throne.

"Silence!" commanded the King, and the great chamber pulsed with the inaudible heartbeats of forty frightened men. The King gripped the throne's armrests and nodded. "Summon the Sorcerer."

The great doors swung open, and a meek voice could be heard saying, "You may go in now, your Protectorate . . . er . . . Protecterness . . . er . . . sir."

Through the grand doorway strode the Sorcerer, cloaked and hooded. With a quick sweep of his eyes he surveyed the entire scene, then approached the King. The swordsmen tensed. Ten feet before the regent he bowed deeply and fell to one knee. "How may I be of service to you, my liege?" boomed the confident, half-mocking voice which emanated from the shadowy depths beneath his hood. No one dared ask him to remove his cloak.

"Well . . . ah," the King began, feeling even less confident than he had just a moment earlier. "It's about my boy, the Prince. He didn't seem quite right there for a while, you know? But I think he's better now."

The Prince, standing by himself a few feet off to the side,

smiled.

"And are you blaming me for this?" The statement was as much accusation as inquiry.

The King looked down at his pink hands, wishing very much that he had never summoned the dreadful wizard into his presence. "Not really blaming . . . ," he mumbled.

"You have heard, have you not," the Sorcerer began in a low, but compelling voice, "the rumors of my powers?"

"Yes." The King's reply was brittle, his mouth dry.

"You've heard of the supernatural occurrences on the mountain where I live?" The Sorcerer's voice grew in volume and majesty as he spoke. "You know of the vile scourge that racked your enemies years ago even as they were about to defile this kingdom and visit total ruin upon you? You know that even now your enemies fear to war against your realm, not because of your insignificant military forces, but because they cower before the loathsome conjurings which *I* might summon up to confront them?"

"Yes." The King did not look up.

"You *owe* me, your highness, for the protection of your kingdom all these years." The throne room throbbed with a queasy silence. "I have answered your summons here today in order to collect."

Fear twisted the King's insides, and half rising, he protested, "But this is your home, too, and you've had your pension . . . . Besides . . . ."

"Yes?" the Sorcerer probed. "Besides what?"

"Well . . . nothing, really." The King slumped back onto the throne, his voice trailing off.

The Sorcerer waited.

"It's just that . . . ," the King began again, but couldn't bring himself to finish.

"It's just that you don't know whether my powers are real or merely a trick? Is that it?"

Wanly the King nodded, averting his gaze.

In the nervous quiet that followed, some feared the King had gone too far in questioning the wizard's potency. The Sorcerer rose from his knees to his full height, a flagrant breach of etiquette which no one seemed to notice nor cared to correct. Though still seated on the high dais, the King felt that the Sorcerer was towering over him and might strike him dead before his soldiers could even flinch.

"Clear the throne room," the magician commanded, "and I shall prove my powers to you alone!"

The King hesitated, more frightened to be alone with the Sorcerer than of anything else his simple mind could imagine at that moment. Yet there was obviously great danger if he failed to comply. He was too confused to act.

The Sorcerer raised his arms, turned in a slow circle, and commanded, "Be gone! All of you! Your King wills it!"

When the King failed to protest, the attendants and petty advisors, then the soldiers standing in open ranks, shuffled, took a few tentative steps, gathered momentum, then stampeded through the grand doors. Two archers peered out uneasily from behind the drapes, wondering if the royal command was intended to include them as well.

"Your archers, too, your highness," the Sorcerer said. "Order them out also."

The King was stunned that the wizard could apparently see through the thick draperies. *What powers this man must have!* he thought wildly. "Out!" he stammered. "All of you out! Can't you obey a simple royal command?"

The hitherto hidden archers stumbled over each other to flee the throne room and its terrible visitor. The giant doors thundered closed behind them.

The Prince, whose fate seemed so integrally bound up in the outcome of the encounter, remained as its only witness. Unlike the others, he feared no harm from the magician, but harbored an amused admiration for his audacity and cleverness.

"And now, for you alone, I shall demonstrate my powers." Slowly the Sorcerer approached the cowering King. He reached beneath his cloak and deftly produced something in his right hand.

"No, please . . . ," the King whimpered. Then he saw it was only a deck of cards. He sat up, his curiosity overcoming his terror as the wizard expertly fanned the deck.

"Take a card, any card. Don't tell me what it is."

Slowly the King complied. The Sorcerer winked at the Prince while the King studied his card.

"Put the card back anywhere in the deck," the Sorcerer instructed, again fanning the cards face down before him.

Once more the King complied.

The wizard held the deck at arm's length, closed it slowly, tapped the top card, and with his eyes shut incanted, "*Onomatopoeia quantum prepuce!*" He turned over the top card, the three-of-cups, and displayed it to the King.

"My God!" cried the King of Nod, as amazed and delighted as a five-year-old. "How did you do that? The three-of-cups was my card!"

"Of course it was," the Sorcerer confirmed placidly, returning the magical deck beneath his cloak. He squared himself before the seated King, eyes burning, his voice a club, coldly bludgeoning the regent with his overwhelming power. "You will grant my single request." It was clearly not a question.

"Yes, of course," whispered the King, averting his gaze, turning sideways, and gripping his fine robes tightly about his neck as if preparing to suffer a mortal blow. "What is it you wish?"

"Your son, the Prince."

Excitement exploded through the Prince like a jolt of lightning, but he tried not to betray it. He struggled to maintain his mask of distant amusement.

"My son? The Prince?" The King looked up bewildered. "What do you want with *him*?"

"I want you to give him your leave to come study under me, and, after studying the ways of sorcery and learning to command its unspeakable and irresistible powers, your leave for him to follow the path of sorcery if he so chooses."

"And what if he doesn't?"

"If he freely chooses not to follow the way of sorcery, after learning it fully, the decision shall be his alone, and I will honor it absolutely. On this you have my word. He may return to the castle or go anywhere else he pleases, as far as I'm concerned. In any event, I shall consider your debt to be fully discharged."

The King was suspicious, but as he thought the proposal over, he visibly relaxed, the fear dropping from his body like ripe fruit. After gazing for a while at the Prince, who still appeared indifferent to the entire prospect, he smiled. "If he learns the powers of which you speak, yet still decides to return to this his home to assist us, and ultimately to inherit the throne, would he retain these formidable powers?"

"Once such powers are learned, they are never forgotten," the Sorcerer explained. He turned his back on the King and strolled away to give him more room to consider the merits of the proposal. "And if he so chooses," the magician added carefully, "these powers would be available to him in the administration of justice within the kingdom. And for that matter, outside the realm."

The prospect of overwhelming the barbarians just across the borders and adding their land to his kingdom was too much for the King to resist. He grinned, he giggled, he laughed outright. "Take him!" He turned to the Prince. "Go with him, son, and learn. You have our blessings. But come here first so that we may kiss you and seal the grant of this commission."

"Yes father." The Prince approached awkwardly, nearly losing his balance from the seething wonder and excitement rioting within the inner city of his mind.

As the King kissed him on the cheek, he whispered so that the Sorcerer could not hear, "Learn from him, my son! Learn the secret of his powers, and bring them back to this throne! The whole world shall soon bow before us!"

The Prince nodded, rose, and followed the Sorcerer out of the chamber without a backward glance.

CHAPTER ELEVEN

On the Road to the Mountain

For the first time in his life the Prince would be traveling abroad without his usual retinue of attendants, soldiers, and special retainers. The Sorcerer absolutely forbade it. While his stallion was made ready for the long journey, the Heir Apparent bade them each in turn a hasty farewell. It was a tearful occasion. The Prince was about to forego the companionship of trusted servants and friends, and each member of his entourage teetered on the brink of unemployment.

Northward at dawn the two horsemen rode, their steeds heavily provisioned, and each rider wrapped against the cold in the cloak of a common wayfarer. The fanfare and cheering which usually attended departures of state was missing, having likewise been forbidden by the wizard. Quietly the journey began. The Prince pondered with nostalgia the closing of a great chapter in his life, and the opening of another, unknown and exciting. Off they rode beneath an overcast sky as obscure as his future.

The Sorcerer seemed tense, afraid that the King might have a last minute change of heart, ever alert for signs of a surreptitious betrayal from an unknown quarter. When the Prince tried to ask him questions about the secret powers of sorcery or the authenticity of strange tales of wonderment whispered around the castle when he was a child, the wizard's responses were terse and cryptic.

They made camp early the first day. The Sorcerer sat up for most of the night watching while the Prince suffered a fitful sleep beside the glowing coals of the evening's campfire. They arose early next morning under the black, starless mantle of low clouds, ate a quick meal of bread and cheese, and were mounted and on their way before daylight had completely filtered in to illuminate their pathway through the ragged foothills. The sky remained gray and menacing, and a cold northeastern gust carried occasional drops of rain into their faces.

After a while they rode over a hillock that stood just south of a broad plain. Ahead of them the road shot straight away into the lingering darkness like the northward flight of a great arrow. On the roadway below they could see the figure of a lone traveler proceeding their same direction on foot. The Sorcerer grew wary as they approached, but the solitary wayfarer was only an old man, his hoary head bobbing beside a long crooked staff, making his feeble progress with painful, tottering steps.

Suddenly the Prince recognized him and galloped on ahead. "Grimm!" he shouted as he reined up his horse and leapt from the saddle. "What are you doing out here?" He embraced the befuddled old man.

When Grimm finally recognized him, he bowed deeply. "Your majesty."

"What are you doing out here?" the Prince insisted. "Where are you going? Why are you traveling all alone? Have you had anything to eat? Do you know that they're worried sick about you back at the castle?"

"I have a mission," the erstwhile Chief Advisor explained slowly. "I am traveling through the countryside warning people. God is very angry. Beware, things are not as they seem."

Just then the Sorcerer drew abreast, and Grimm looked up, recognizing him instantly. In great terror and agitation he tore free from the Prince's grasp. Like a palsied puppet jerked suddenly upright by a wire through its skull, Grimm straightened, shaking violently, and spun around as if in the throes of a grand mal seizure, his eyes rolling back into his head and his tongue lolling out of the side of his mouth. He twirled and spun, balancing on outstretched toes like an epileptic ballerina, emitted a high warbling rattle intended to be "Hosanna!" and then, as if the wire had been suddenly severed, pitched forward on his face in the middle of the dusty roadway, assuming a position of the most abject submission before the bewildered horse and rider. He lay there motionless.

The Prince stepped carefully over to the Sorcerer and whispered, "It's Grimm."

"Ah, yes," the wizard whispered back, dismounting. "The King's Chief Advisor. I knew him. What's the problem?"

"My father says that he believes you're God."

"Ah." The Sorcerer tied the reins of his horse to the low branch of a scrub oak beside the road and walked over to the prostrate figure. "It's all right, old man. You can get up now."

Grimm did not move.

The magician thought for a moment. "All is forgiven. I hereby grant you a joyful afterlife of eternal bliss. But arise now, please, and look at me."

Still Grimm did not move.

The Prince knelt down to help him up, but when he touched the ancient shoulders, the hoary head flopped over on its cheek. Grimm's face was a puffy, oxygen-starved blue, and his sightlessly staring eyes had already begun to glaze over. The Prince recoiled in horror. He had never seen a dead man before.

While the Sorcerer struggled futilely to revive him, the Prince paced back and forth in the dust, wringing his hands. "What happened to him?" he asked at last.

The wizard sat back in the dirt and drew a deep breath, abandoning his fruitless efforts. "It looks to me like his poor old heart just couldn't stand the excitement of a face-to-face encounter with his Maker."

Having lived his entire life with a retainer for every chore, the Prince could not begin to imagine what one did with a corpse. The Sorcerer, however, seemed to know. So the Prince helped him carry Grimm's stiffening carcass to a small stream where they washed it carefully. Fond recollections of the living old man swam through his mind as they worked. Then they wrapped the cadaver in a clean sheet from the wizard's bedroll and draped it over the rump of the Prince's stallion, where it looked like a huge forsaken cocoon, the butterfly of life having flown merrily on its way.

At a nearby village they consigned their macabre package to a local mortician, instructing him to return it at once to the castle for a

funeral of state. Their task completed, the magician and his royal
conscript returned to the great north-south highway and rode in silence
for the rest of the day, as if death itself had joined their party as an
invisible third horseman who wished not to be disturbed.

Next morning the sun rose bright and clear. The warm
sunshine and blue sky helped to dissipate the previous day's horror.
Birds sang happily from the branches and bushes.

About midday they turned from the royal highway onto the
ragged, overgrown trail that led off to the east towards the Sorcerer's
mountain. When they had ridden out of sight of the main road and it
appeared that no one was in pursuit, the Sorcerer threw back his hood.
He looked somewhat older, thinner, a bit more ordinary, slightly less
majestic than the Prince had first perceived him.

"Would you like to know why I chose you?" The magician
smiled warmly over his shoulder.

"Yes." The Prince spurred his horse up close behind the older
man's. "Please tell me." He was glad to be conversing at last.

"Because you have been asking the right questions, young
man."

"I have?"

"Yes. And I believe you'll be able to grasp the awful secrets
of sorcery without crumbling beneath the sheer weight of the truth."
He chuckled to himself for a moment, but he did not share the joke
with his young companion.

The Prince decided to try a different subject. "I'm looking
forward to seeing the unicorn," he called out happily.

The Sorcerer turned around awkwardly in the saddle. "The
what?"

"The unicorn."

"What unicorn?"

"Why, you have a unicorn, don't you?"

"No," the Sorcerer replied. "I've never seen a unicorn in my
life. Don't believe in them." He faced forward again.

The Prince probed his memory carefully. After a while he
called out again, "I remember your sending a message to my father,

the King, when I was still a boy. He had invited you to the castle. You replied that you couldn't come because your unicorn was sick and needed your close attention. It's one of my earliest recollections."

"Oh, that." The Sorcerer pulled his horse out upon a small rocky flat just above a sharp switchback in the trail. "Yes, I remember sending that message now. For your father I have a unicorn. But for you I do not."

The Prince reined up just below him on the trail. "Which is the truth? Do you have a unicorn or not?"

"Do you mean the truth for you? Or the truth for your father?"

The Prince's pout was that of a little boy about to burst into tears at an older child's teasing.

The Sorcerer laughed. "For your father, I have great powers. I can make a card move through a solid deck. Here." He pulled the deck of cards from a pocket in his robe and, reaching down, handed it to the younger man. "Examine these carefully."

The Prince took the cards and fanned them open. To his amazement, and then amusement, he discovered that every card was an identical three-of-cups.

"For you," the wizard explained, "these powers are no longer nearly so magical nor profound. Therein lies the truth." He dug his heels into his steed's abdomen and leapt ahead up the trail.

The pathway narrowed and the horses began the slow climb single-file up the steep face of the escarpment, the Sorcerer in the lead. As the way became ever more difficult, further discussion grew all but impossible.

It was late afternoon, with much of the steep climb behind them and the peak looming overhead, when the Sorcerer turned off the main trail into a small, flat wooded glen where a spring in the side of the mountain gushed forth clear, cold water. Below it, a series of musical cascades led to a small pool, and a slender silver stream snaked its way from the pool to the edge of the precipice, then tumbled down the rocky cliff face through a bottomless haze of wind-blown spray. On the western side of the pool a lawn of short grass and moss spread, with great shimmering white granite rocks towering here and there in the green landscape like flinty sentries guarding the mountain's western flank. A few gnarled cedars clung with twisted roots to the rocks along the stream bank.

"This is one of my favorite places," the Sorcerer said as he dismounted. He tucked the reins into the horse's leather harness and allowed the weary beast to graze freely in the lush oasis. He knelt down beside the pool, splashed water on his face and neck, and drank deeply from cupped hands. "Drink your fill," he advised the Prince. He pulled an apple from somewhere in his robes and deftly sliced it in half with his knife. "We won't eat again until we arrive home this evening. Except for this." He handed one piece to his companion.

The Prince refreshed himself in the cold water, then sat down and ate the tart fruit. He lay back contented on the dry grass in the warm afternoon sunlight beneath an ancient cedar and gazed off into the distance. "What's that?" he asked, pointing lazily toward a snow-covered peak that seemed to shimmer above the hazy horizon without touching it.

The Sorcerer followed his gaze. "Those are the mountains of Ararat."

The Prince stretched his tired legs and sat up. "Why the mushrooms?" he asked.

"Why not?" the wizard replied. "The time has to be filled somehow." A small blue-violet flower growing from the mossy soil between two huge rocks had caught his eye. He bent forward to study it, ignoring the more gaudy tiger lilies that crowded around the tinkling stream like haughty ladies in speckled bonnets gossiping at an afternoon tea.

"Was there a lesson I was to learn from them?" the Prince persisted.

"There is always a lesson, in every experience." The Sorcerer plucked the tiny blossom and twirled it thoughtfully between his thumb and finger. "This seems to be some sort of penstemon, I think. I haven't seen one quite like this before. I think I'll call it 'sorcererswort'. It might have some interesting pharmaceutical potential."

"I felt that I had finally grasped the absolute truth," the Prince confessed, ignoring the botanical discovery. "When I took the last portion of mushrooms. But now I can't remember with any precision the certainty I experienced."

The Sorcerer sighed and placed the sample of sorcererswort carefully into a pocket of his robe. He leaned back and looked at his pupil. "You use the words 'truth' and 'certainty' as if they were referring to the same subject. This is a mistake, for the concepts are very different. Certainty is a feeling, an emotional state, like fear or love, horror or melancholy. A simple syllogism or a mathematical equation can generate certainty. Three times nine equals twenty-seven. Of this I feel certain, though I do not every time count the twenty-seven objects to confirm my feeling. If I do actually count, the certainty is reinforced if it comes out right, but if it does not, then certainty disappears. Mushrooms can also generate this feeling of certainty. I don't know how or why, I just know that they can. Whatever patterns of reality or connections of thought are present at just such a time are perceived with certainty."

"And this feeling of certainty allows us to grasp the truth?"

"The truth is there all the time, within us, whether we grasp it or not. You don't need mushrooms to find it."

The Prince rubbed his chin. "What is the truth, then?"

The wizard laughed and lay back on the grass. "Your approach is very direct, young man." He sat up slowly, thoughtfully, searching for precisely the right words. "The truth is like a crystal with infinite facets suspended in mid-air. What you see in the crystal depends upon what is refracted and reflected back to your particular point of view. We all see the same crystal, but because no two of us can occupy exactly the same viewpoint at the same time, we each see a different truth."

The Prince shook his head in frustration. "But what of the *absolute* truth?"

"We each of us perceive absolute truth, beyond denial, incontrovertible. But move slightly, and a different truth presents itself absolutely. The whole world in all its infinite detail is precisely refracted in the crystal of truth in various patterns and permutations. Our shortcoming is that we can only view it from one angle at a time."

"Then the crystal itself is the absolute truth, isn't it?"

"No. The crystal is itself empty of all content."

The Prince wrestled with the elusive concept for a while, then announced decisively, "Well, I want to see all the truths, all at the same time."

"Then you will have to become the crystal, reflecting everything, empty of yourself."

They both fell silent. The horses tore up and chewed the rich grass, wind whispered through the cedars, and the magical song of the waterfalls filled the clear air. After a while the Sorcerer began to speak in a soft, reflective tone that harmonized perfectly with the other sounds of nature. "Your quest for absolute certainty is hardly unique or unusual. It springs from a restlessness which is fundamental to consciousness. Each time another sentient being is conceived and born, the innermost layers of being are somehow pried apart and a tiny bubble of nothingness is inserted in the something, like the grain of sand that irritates the oyster's tender flesh. The universe is suddenly awake, aware of itself, however dimly. Consciousness discovers itself to be other, separate from that which it contemplates, and it longs to heal the breach, to be reunited once again. For you this yearning translates itself into the quest for certainty."

"Then why do I feel so alone in my search?"

"No two paths are precisely the same. They all lead to the same destination, but their courses diverge. Most people find tricks to assuage their emptiness. Some project their need onto the physical interplay of things in the world. Others use religion, a belief in the Absolute, to produce the certainty they crave. Still others cling to a guiding principle, like the sheer accumulation of wealth, to which they become mindless servants."

"Where do the paths all lead?"

"How should I know?" the wizard laughed. "I haven't been to the end of mine yet."

"Has anyone?"

"Oh my, yes."

"Who?"

"Grimm, for one."

"So Grimm now knows the truth? Is that what you're saying?"

"No. Grimm knows nothing now. He *is* the truth. Or a part of it, like this rock and that tree. Ultimately the little bubble of nothingness pops, as it did with Grimm, and the disjointed layers meld back together into a fundamental sleeping oneness which is not different from the truth. The question no longer arises. In the end, it all comes to the same thing."

The "caw" of a crow departing the cedar under which the Prince sat added a final punctuation to the wizard's words.

"It's time to move on," the Sorcerer declared, arising.

The Prince pondered the strange new ideas as he caught his chestnut stallion and mounted. "But this means," he suddenly burst out, "this means that the feeling of certainty isn't a reliable measure for judging between conflicting truths. One man's truth is just as good as another's."

"Congratulations," said the Sorcerer as he spurred his mount back onto the main trail. "You have just mastered the first lesson."

The sun had already set when they rode over the crest of the last ridge and descended into the darkness engulfing the magician's homestead. Both men were tired and hungry. They dismounted at the small stable beyond the cottage and were unsaddling their horses when a woman appeared out of the shadows carrying an oil lamp before her.

"Ah, Manat," the Sorcerer said fondly. "The Prince will be staying with us for a while. Please look after him. We'll be taking our meals together in the kitchen." He turned to the Prince. "Manat has been with me for years. She can be trusted and will do the chores which would otherwise require your attention."

The Prince looked her over as she raised the oil lamp and, stretching on her tiptoes, hung it from a nail sticking out of one of the low rafters. Appearing neither young nor old, she was so slender he could see the skeletal structure beneath her brown skin. Her thin face was plain, but scarred and pocked from a childhood disease. Manat was definitely not the black-haired woman he had seen through the kitchen door on his last visit, which now seemed long, long ago. He was disappointed.

"It's a pleasure to meet you, Manat." The Prince extended his hand as to a lady of rank.

Shivering in the evening chill, Manat stepped out from beneath the bright light. She lowered her eyes and curtsied slightly, but did not take his hand. Immediately she set about the tasks of feeding and currying the tired horses.

"Tomorrow we will begin," the Sorcerer announced as they walked along the dark path to the cottage. A lamp burning in the kitchen window beckoned like a star lost in the void of intergalactic space.

"Begin what? What do you have in mind for me?"

"I think some day you may inherit my place, young man. And the royal blood flowing through your veins won't hurt you a bit when it comes to making believers out of the rest of them."

The Prince's brow was knit. "The citizens of the realm?"

"Yes. And the barbarians beyond the borders, too, our most important audience." The magician chuckled. "Be patient, my boy. You'll learn the truth soon enough. Tonight let us rest and eat a hearty meal."

"As condemned men?" the Prince quipped.

"As men who are about to undertake a difficult journey into an unknown wasteland." The Sorcerer smiled and held open the kitchen door.

CHAPTER TWELVE

The Truth of Sorcery

The next morning, after groat clusters, fried yams, and sweet goat's milk cheese, the Prince and the Sorcerer sat finishing up honeyed scones and gingerroot tea. Manat had cleared away the rest of the breakfast dishes and could be heard humming softly to herself in the next room as she washed up. Her efficiency, her silent, direct manner, her contentment with simple chores reminded the Prince of Brother Widgeon and the devoted monks he had met at the monastery.

"I thought about it last night," the Sorcerer was saying as he dunked his scone in the spicy tea, "and I've decided it would be best if I made known to you right from the beginning what I perceive to be the truth of this sorcery business." He bit carefully into the dripping scone. "I suspect that you will not completely believe what I am about to tell you. I was as enthusiastic as you once many years ago, so I understand your sentiments. Rest assured, however, that you will have plenty of time to confirm or disprove these matters to you own satisfaction."

The Prince quietly set down his teacup. "What do you perceive to be the truth of sorcery?"

"That my search for magical power has been fruitless. Utterly in vain."

"But, surely–"

With a wave of his hand he cut the Prince off. "Please, let me finish." He drank off the rest of his tea and set the empty cup on his plate. "Some thirty-odd years ago, as a young man just about your age now, I came here to study sorcery. I had come into possession of the secret tomes written by sorcerers, truth seekers, alchemists, magicians, and assorted necromancers since the beginning of time. These books fell into my hands through such a bizarre and fortuitous series of events that I was convinced I had somehow been chosen to carry the fire as custodian of their darkest secrets and as successor to the limitless powers they promised. I won't go into the story of how I came by these books now. Perhaps another day." He blotted his lips with his napkin, folded it neatly, and laid it beside his plate. "Suffice it to say that I had, and still have, every volume ever written on the subject, and their authenticity is beyond question." The Sorcerer nodded to the low doorway at the back of the kitchen. "You will have ample opportunity to examine these strange books for yourself and try your hand at sorcery, all in good time."

The Prince gazed thoughtfully at the small door, recalling the dusty disorder of antique volumes and countless bins, vials, drawers, jars, bottles, and strange instruments that he had encountered the last time he had passed through into the low chamber on the other side. His mind conjured for the ten-thousandth time a vision of the raven-haired woman slipping silently back through the passageway. The intertwined recollections excited him.

"I didn't come here alone. My young wife and I . . . 'Sarai' was her name . . . Sarai and I spent a good many years perusing those volumes, following instructions, translating formulae, gathering herbs and roots, collecting bark and beetles, haunting hidden stalls down secret corridors of foreign markets to purchase rare elements and ancient mixtures. Have you ever considered how very difficult it is to find fresh cobra venom or locate samples of that certain fungus that only grows on dried giraffe droppings?"

The Prince shook his head.

"Well, anyway, Sarai and I tried everything. We experimented with every imaginable spell, incanted magic phrases until our throats were sore, and dabbled in all conceivable extremes of magical conjuring, black, white, and every shade in between. In the end, I had to conclude that none of the ancient secrets are worth the crumbling paper they're written on, none of the formulae work, and the entire field of sorcery is at best a trick and at worst a cruel fraud."

The Prince felt like he had just had the wind knocked out of him. Such a startling confession from the mighty Sorcerer was something he had not been prepared for. Suddenly he laughed nervously. "Surely you're joking. Is this a trick?"

The Sorcerer was not joking. It was no trick.

"Perhaps the experiments were not performed properly. You may have overlooked some critical step."

"No. We tried them over and over again with endless variations. Nothing worked."

"But what of your defense of the kingdom!" cried the Prince. "What of the barbarian armies that you destroyed before they could set foot inside the realm? You claimed responsibility for that! You accepted the highest honors bestowed by the King!"

"In a way, I *was* responsible." The Sorcerer hung his head and made it sound like a curse, not a heroic deed. "But the victory was not brought about by supernatural power."

"How then? Tell me!"

The older man remained silent for a long time, collecting his thoughts, coming to grips with painful memories. He did not look up when he finally spoke. "In the early days Sarai and I had hoped by means of conjuring to be able to call back from the dead a child who had fallen to the filthy disease smallpox. We still believed in the awesome powers of sorcery at that time. An essential ingredient in that particular spell was the diseased tissue from the dead child, which I had obtained with some difficulty. We kept the foul culture alive in a petri dish on a thick broth of chicken soup while we tried to perfect the other elements of the spell. It was dangerous, of course, keeping the vile growth on hand, but we were extremely careful with it."

The Sorcerer looked up at the Prince. "You were very young and probably don't remember too clearly the time when the barbarian armies of Jabal the Chosen massed at our borders, threatening to invade this kingdom and overwhelm us with murder, rape, torture, and anarchy. There was hysteria throughout the realm, and no one seemed to be able to do anything. Our army was small and without adequate equipment, supplies, or, for that matter, leadership, to defend itself or anyone else."

The Prince bristled at the reference to the King's lack of leadership, although he knew that the judgment was probably justified.

"Sarai and I debated what should be done. She felt that the smallpox preserved in the tissue sample should be spread among the invaders. It would surely decimate their ranks before a single battle was joined. I argued that it was too horrible a weapon, even for the worst of enemies. Besides, I could think of no safe vehicle by which the disease could be introduced among the enemy in time. It was our only hope of salvation, yet it seemed to be a fantastic and fruitless dream."

Manat came softly into the room, and the wizard fell silent. She cleared away the remaining plates and teacups and then retreated quietly.

The Prince urged gently, "Please, go on."

"Sarai figured out a way to spread the loathsome disease." A shiver passed through the Sorcerer. "She never spoke of what she planned to do. She knew I wouldn't approve. She did what she felt she had to. I awoke one morning and she was gone. The petri dish that contained the smallpox culture was empty. Beside it was a note from Sarai telling me what she intended to do, what she had already done. Beside myself with grief, I saddled my horse and rode after her, though I knew it was already too late. At the main highway I met some of your father's soldiers. They had been sent to summon me to the castle to help the King in his confrontation with messengers from the barbarians. I told them I couldn't go with them. I must have raved like a lunatic. I don't remember clearly. They clamped me in irons and hauled me to the castle like a common criminal." He picked up his napkin and dabbed at his moist eyes. "I never saw Sarai again."

The Prince waited silently for the Sorcerer to continue.

"Sarai had of course infected herself with the smallpox," the wizard murmured at last. "She was able to move freely among the enemy troops. Oh, what a lovely woman she was! I can assure you she had no trouble passing from camp to camp--" The Sorcerer dropped his eyes, and his voice grew faint. "She personally infected key units of that filthy horde, a few minutes of contact with a soldier here perhaps, an evening with an officer there . . . ." He drew a deep breath and looked up at the Prince. "Within a fortnight, the enemy was destroyed."

The Prince was stunned. "But you claimed credit for the rout--"

"Yes! Dear God, not for myself! I wanted nothing more than that the truth be known. Sarai should have been immortalized for her sacrifice. She deserves the honor and tribute of this entire nation. And yet I had to weigh her honor against the survival of this kingdom. She was gone forever, and honor would no longer do her any good. But by claiming the responsibility myself . . . .

"I formulated my plan almost as soon as I knew what she had done. It seemed so obvious. Before the disease showed itself among the enemy troops, I issued my well-remembered threat to their loathsome messenger Barth. I ordained that a great infestation would destroy his army, just as it did. My stratagem worked. They believe that I, as mighty Sorcerer and invincible Protector of the Kingdom, possess terrible powers against which all force is futile. That's the sole reason the barbarians leave us alone."

The Prince was moved by the story, but he was also deeply troubled. "Everyone believes in your great powers. The enemy fears them. The whole kingdom relies on them. I grew up trusting in them. And now you say it's all been a trick." He looked the magician straight in the eye. "I came here to learn those powers! This is important to me!"

The Sorcerer returned his gaze implacably.

"What do you want from me, then?" the Prince asked.

"I'm growing old. My health isn't what it used to be. I can't keep the enemy armies at bay forever by myself. I'll need a successor."

"Successor to what! You just told me you haven't the magical power to defend the kingdom from an aroused pussycat, let alone a rabid horde of spear-wielding savages! If what you say is true, what can a successor do?"

"Nothing. But like me, he can possess the *appearance* of absolute power. That appearance alone will serve as an absolute deterrent to aggression."

"I'm not sure what to believe," the Prince moaned as he stood and walked over to the window. He pressed his forehead against the cool pane.

The Sorcerer arose slowly and laid a hand gently on the younger man's shoulder. "Enough of this for now. You'll have plenty of time to contemplate these matters and reach your own conclusions. Let me show you the laboratory and my exquisite collection of ancient, but, alas, impotent, tomes."

They spent the rest of the day poking through the laboratory, opening this volume or that, probing through drawers of strange mixtures, bottles of exotic chemicals, and jars of rare and mysterious compounds, from crushed cactus buttons to extract of boll weevil, and from datura seeds to roots of the devil's weed. The wizard did his best to answer his pupil's questions about the various chemicals, potions, unguents, brews, and balms and their uses in the dark sciences.

"I've attempted to keep most of the staple ingredients fresh and current," sighed the Sorcerer as he wrinkled his nose at a small jar containing the fat from a stillborn baby which had undoubtedly gone rancid. "I must admit my diligence has suffered a bit in the last few years." He made an entry on a small tablet he was carrying.

"Can we get more?"

"Oh, we'll have no trouble collecting most of these things ourselves. In fact, I think a little gathering expedition will be an enlightening aspect of your training." He referred to his tablet. "Let's see. Enchanter's nightshade, wild lettuce, wolf's foot, fly agaric if we're lucky, wolfsbane, and perhaps even hemlock and morning glory seeds should be no problem."

"What about that?" The Prince pointed to the malodorous jar in the magician's hand.

"This? This is more of a problem. It will have to be purchased from the right source. As will fresh vampire bat blood. Ours has congealed. And the skin of a rare toad that lives in a tropical climate. And a number of other items are going to require my visiting a few old friends whom I haven't seen in years. I'll make the trip after you feel a little more comfortable here by yourself. You'll probably need all these things for your attempts at conjuring, if you decide to give it a try."

"I do want to try," the Prince announced decisively. "I want to study these ancient writings and try to work some of the spells myself."

"Of course. That is the very choice I would have made if I were in your position. We can put things in order this afternoon, and you can begin tomorrow."

After a quick inventory, the first major task was to clean and sweep the long-neglected room and restore some semblance of order. They dusted everything and placed volumes that had lain open for years back into the shelves where they belonged. As he worked, the Prince kept constantly vigilant for any sign of *her*, but from all appearances the room had not been occupied for many years.

Later that night, long after the faint crescent moon had smothered itself in the twilit western horizon and a star-emblazoned blackness had settled on the mountain, the Sorcerer wheeled out a wobbly old barrow with a small vat tethered inside. He carefully measured several volatile ingredients into the vat and mixed them thoroughly with the long handle from a broken shovel. Then he rolled the rickety vehicle up the hill and onto a flat, fire-charred clearing defined by a closed circle of blackened stones. He poured the contents out onto the sooty ground.

"Stand back," he warned the Prince as he went to the cottage to fetch a torch. When he returned, he pitched the flaming stick into the mixture, which exploded into blazing orange flames, punctuated by belching prominences of red and bright blue. The Sorcerer pointed to the low smoke cloud that hovered overhead, reflecting the changing light in eerie shades of orange, red, and blue, like a giant cotton-candy golf ball stuck atop the mountain. The Sorcerer chuckled. "One has to keep up appearances, after all."

CHAPTER THIRTEEN

The Prince Tries His Hand

The Sorcerer was a gentle teacher and allowed his pupil free rein to explore the matters that interested him, select his own experiments, and make up his own mind about the results. His tutelage was as thorough, conscientious, and spirited as if he himself believed in the truth of the secrets he transmitted. Following the discussion on the first morning after the Prince's arrival, the Sorcerer never again drew into question the efficacy of the discipline. He guided the Prince slowly at first, as a fawning father might encourage the first tentative steps of an infant son, assisting, urging, cajoling, demonstrating wherever possible. Step by step, symbol by symbol, chant by chant, the magician led the younger man through his first few spells, translating specialized terminology, identifying herbs, barks, roots, and oils as they were called for, reciting esoteric incantations over and over again until the Prince had mastered the proper enunciation.

As for the Prince, he clutched the proffered threads of knowledge as a man sinking into quicksand might grasp a wispy branch extended to him. He devoured everything the Sorcerer set before him with the appetite of one who was near starvation. His eyes were those of a voyeur as he watched for signs that the spells were working, his ears those of a siren-struck sailor, deaf to anything that had not the ring of sorcery. Magic seduced his secret thoughts absolutely and held out to him a hope that things might yet turn out all right. So obsessed with his search for the true nature of things did he become, that he neglected his other interests altogether and even abandoned that chamber of his conscious mind which contained the memory of the raven-haired woman, seen fleetingly on his first visit. Unconsciously, however, she wandered freely through every room of his mental house, haunting his mind's entire estate. Indeed, deep within him the search for sorcery and for her had become the same quest.

The spells they attempted were simple ones, designed for instruction and practice only. First the Sorcerer led the Prince through the traditional ceremony, frequently done blindfolded by accomplished wizards of yore, designed to clear the air of evil spirits, and made him repeat it again and again until it was mastered. Whether any baleful spirits had indeed been exorcized, however, was never quite clear. He quickly graduated to the more complicated rite of protecting the fruit trees from hoarfrost at night. No tree damage could be found when the ceremony had been completed, but nights were always balmy that time of year anyway. Then one morning during an unexpected cloudburst they quickly threw together the ingredients for the ritual to stop the rain, which promptly complied. It seemed to the Prince that the downpour had ceased shortly before the rite was consummated, however, and he remained suspicious. The attempt to alter the phases of the moon turned out to be a dismal failure no matter how many times they repeated it.

Faced with such inauspicious results, the Prince began to question his mentor's methods. He wondered, for instance, if they were using accurate translations of the ancient symbols contained in some of the oldest volumes, crumbling tomes with tattered pages bound in decrepit, cracking leather covers. "How do I know these markings have been correctly interpreted?" he asked, pointing to translations scrawled between lines of obscure glyphs and cryptic runes.

"I will show you how we did them, and you may check for yourself." The Sorcerer took down an old dictionary, opened a transliteration index of ancient vintage, and presented the Prince with some worksheets that he himself had compiled when the translations were done.

"I will check them," the Prince replied.

"Take your time. I want you to feel that you have left nothing undone."

"What else could it be?" the Prince wailed. "These things

must have worked for the ones who wrote the books."

"Concentration perhaps," the Sorcerer offered.

"Concentration?"

"Proper concentration is the most fundamental condition precedent for successful sorcery. Or so the ancients tell us. You must silence the constant chattering of your own internal thoughts by centering on the nothingness within you, then let the magic expand by itself to fill every corner of your awareness. Nothing else must exist for you."

So the Prince tried to attain the proper clarity of mind. He began to spend as much time preparing himself, by sitting quietly, thinking of nothing, as he did preparing the ingredients, setting, and incantations for the magic spells. The wonderful peace of mind that sprang up inside reminded him of his attempts at silent, wordless prayer with Brother Widgeon at the monastery. The Sorcerer encouraged the practice of proper concentration even while rooting about in the forest for barks and mushrooms, worms and fungi, which they would do nearly every afternoon. The only words spoken between them on such outings were brief inquiries by the Prince and terse instructions from his tutor.

One evening while alone in the laboratory checking some translations, the Prince came upon an account describing the mystical qualities of a bitter tea brewed from certain ground beans, bark, and leaves from the nightshade plant. The beverage was said to have the ability to facilitate the proper state of concentration, enhancing and deepening it. He rummaged about for the ingredients, prepared the brew, and without bothering to consult the Sorcerer, quaffed down the foul concoction. The ensuing trance-like clarity he found to be salubrious and conducive to a deeper comprehension of the ancient texts. He was astonished that the Sorcerer had not told him about the facilitating beverage.

The next day he asked him about it.

The Sorcerer was greatly disturbed by the Prince's unauthorized consumption of the magic elixir. "These potions can be dangerous," he warned. "You're not ready for them yet. You must gain mastery over yourself first. Otherwise you cannot hope to maintain control. These powers which you call up so lightly will use you for their own terrible purposes if you're not careful."

"I am ready for them. Are there more?"

"You will soon read about others that are yet too dangerous for you. I must warn you away from them. Please consult me before you consume anything else."

The Sorcerer's admonitions only served to whet the Prince's appetite for more. While the wizard was away for a few days in quest of fresh bat blood and fly agaric, which they had been unable to locate in the forest, the Prince scoured the ancient texts for every account he could find of consciousness-enhancing potions, snuffs, unctions, draughts, and powders which he could sip, snort, swallow, or smear on his body. The accounts were numerous. One by one, with enormous patience, he prepared the concoctions and then tried a tiny portion of each just to see what would happen to him. Whenever he read of the chemical properties of a certain root or herb, leaf or fungus, he would seek it out among the bottles, drawers, vials, bins, and vats that filled the laboratory and ingest a small sample just to test the veracity of the written accounts.

Thus while the Sorcerer was away, and with the help of a peculiar flower resin he smoked, the Prince performed what he interpreted to be his first successful magic. The object was to transform raisins into flies. He drew a circle of powdered ox bone on a flat rock in the sunlight, placed seven raisins in the prescribed configuration inside, incanted a string of secret phrases, drew deeply from his pipe, and sat before the circle in a profound trance for more than an hour. When he awoke from the trance, the raisins were gone, and several flies buzzed lazily around three brown pellets lying within the circle.

When the Sorcerer returned, the Prince told him of the magic. He left the smoking of the resin out of his account. He asked his teacher if he could tell him what the pellets were.

The Sorcerer looked at them carefully. "Ground squirrel droppings," he replied. "Congratulations."

With the Sorcerer's return, the Prince found his favorite time to be late at night, long after his teacher had retired, when he was free to study and experiment as he pleased. He spent endless joyful hours within the small glowing circle of the oil lamp which hung over one end of the large oak table in the center of the low room, reading, studying, perusing, learning from the antique volumes and experimenting with the assorted mind-altering substances like condiments at a banquet of the mind. The more he read, the more he wanted to know. He suspected there was an overall order to all of sorcery, and he struggled to comprehend it. He slept later and later into the morning as his studies began to consume the entire night.

Late one evening he happened across a provocative passage in one of the oldest books, praising the limitless powers to be derived from the use of fly agaric. The Prince had not yet experimented with that particular fungus because there had been none available, though he had read of its awesome applications in several places. The Sorcerer had recently replenished the supply, however, and the Prince itched to get at it. He cautiously drew open the appropriate bin and encountered the most ostentatious mushroom he had ever seen. Like fanciful toadstools contrived for a child's fable, a dozen fat specimens lounged in gaudy splendor in the bottom of the drawer, capped in brilliant red and white speckles, fairly glowing up at him.

"My, my, my," he murmured approvingly.

Many of the accounts warned of the poisonous aspect of the strange agaric. The one he had just finished, however, outlined a simple procedure for detoxifying the fungus and at the same time enhancing the potency of the resulting potion. With enormous care and reverence the Prince lifted one of the bright mushrooms out of the bin, tore it into tiny pieces, and mixed it with the prescribed complement of herbs, roots, and leaves into a small kettle of boiling water. When the mixture had cooled and solidified, he divided it into eight equal portions, eating one quickly and saving the rest for another time. In the dark, still hours that followed, alone with the night, he poked about the laboratory watching and waiting for whatever strange effects might manifest themselves.

In the space between two cabinets he discovered a great, heavy volume entitled "Synoptic Index of Alchemical Writings" half hidden behind a stack of other books, as if it had been intentionally concealed there. Inside was a handwritten abstract of the other tomes surrounding him, with careful references to each. The entire library had been painstakingly systematized and condensed into this one volume which now contained a coherent expression of the essence of sorcery. So fascinated did the Prince become with this new discovery that he completely forgot the powerful potion he had consumed.

After he had read avidly for a long while, the Prince grew slowly aware of a feeling that someone else was in the room with him. He looked up and beheld at the far end of the long table, seated just barely within the glow of the lamp, mostly still in shadow, the beautiful dark-haired woman he had seen months earlier. She sat quietly and watched him with unhurried amusement. Her skin was white as milk, her hair jet black, flowing straight upon her shoulders and down her back. She wore a black robe decorated with small, white crescent moons. Around her neck was a sparkling chain with a silver medallion in the same crescent shape which flashed with the reflected fire of the oil lamp when she turned. Serenely she smiled at him, but spoke not a word. The lines of her face were sculpted with incredible simplicity and loveliness. They gazed at each other thus for a long time.

The Prince was neither abashed to find himself watched, nor disconcerted by her stunning beauty. Instead, a dreamlike peace and a sense of total appropriateness filled him. "I feel I have invaded your place," he said at last. "Forgive me."

She smiled in acknowledgment and nodded slightly, her eyes flashing like the medallion.

"I am the Prince." He did not stand up, as good manners would dictate. He knew she would understand with an understanding beyond good manners. "I had hoped you would come."

"I have come to help you learn," she replied softly, her voice like the whisper of the wind in the trees. "If you will allow me, there is much I can teach you."

"I wish nothing else but to learn from you." He gazed into the infinite depths of her eyes. Within him the Prince felt a strange completeness filling a place he had never before perceived as empty.

"Sorcery is but a mirror," she murmured, binding his gaze to hers. "You can find in it whatever you allow yourself. That my father could not find the limitless power he once sought is merely a reflection of him, nothing more. To possess sorcery completely, to tap its vast powers, you must give yourself completely." Her perfect smile hinted of an irony he could not comprehend. "Are you ready to give yourself completely?"

"Yes." He responded without hesitation. He felt as though he stood at the threshold of a gateway through which he was destined to pass, indeed, had secretly longed to pass his entire life without even knowing it was there. Without pause he gave himself utterly to the open portal and to the pathway beyond, just barely glimpsed, because for him there was no longer any other way.

"Then mark this as the beginning." Her crescent medallion flashed. "And forget everything else that has gone before."

"How do I begin?"

"Study these books." She opened her arms in a graceful arc that encompassed the entire library. Her hands were as white as her face and soared like doves dancing a perfectly choreographed accompaniment to her words. "And learn from these chemicals and potions. I will be here whenever you need me to help unlock the most difficult secrets. You need not call. I will be watching and will know when you are in need of me. I only ask one thing of you for now." Her gaze held him captive. "You must swear not to say anything to my father about this meeting."

"Why shouldn't he know?"

"Swear you will not."

"But why?"

"Swear it."

There was much the Prince did not understand, but he knew he had to trust her unquestioningly if he was to succeed in the mastery of sorcery. "I swear it."

"The volume you have before you is the key. When you find yourself in doubt, return to it."

The Prince examined the Synoptic Index more closely. It appeared to be in much better condition than the other volumes. It was divided into sections on sorcery, magic, alchemy, and metaphysics.   All the other tomes in the library seemed to be carefully cross-referenced and summarized. Surprisingly, most of the chapters ended with a series of empty pages, as if the author had intended to add to them.   The Prince realized that the volume he held was unfinished, was even now in the process of being written.

"You are writing this–?" he began to ask, but when he looked up, she was gone. Without dismay, but with the purposefulness of a pilgrim fulfilling a sacred vow, he redoubled the intensity of his study.

CHAPTER FOURTEEN

The Truth of Sorcery, Another View

Next afternoon the Prince disclosed to the Sorcerer that he had located the Synoptic Index and was now studying it, to see what his mentor's reaction might be. The magician expressed his great pleasure, for the volume had been misplaced for some time. It seemed to the Prince, however, that he was holding something back.

"It's a beautifully written book," the Prince pressed.

"Yes." The Sorcerer grew reflective. "It was written by a beautiful hand." He volunteered no more.

"Did you ever have any children?" the Prince blurted out, and then bit his tongue, for he was flirting with a breach of his sacred vow not to reveal his meeting with the Sorcerer's daughter. The wizard looked at him curiously, and it seemed to the Prince that the older man wondered how much he knew about the book's authorship.

"My wife and I had a daughter shortly after we arrived here." The Sorcerer offered no more on the subject, but the Prince's inquiry seemed to trouble him somehow.

Despite his better judgment, the Prince might have pressed his interrogation even further had Manat not knocked and announced that a lone horseman was approaching from the west. It was a royal messenger from the King inquiring after the Prince's health and the progress of his studies. He conveyed the King's invitation to come to the castle for a short vacation and a visit with his father.

The Prince declined brusquely. His fledgling studies had only begun. Besides, he had no time to spare just now.

The messenger reminded him that he had already been with the Sorcerer eight weeks and had not sent a single message to his anxious father.

"Eight weeks!" the Prince marveled. "Could so much time have gone by already?" He nonetheless bade the messenger carry his regrets to the King, but he thought it best to decline the royal invitation at just this time. "Another time. Soon."

That evening the Prince plunged with increased urgency into the study of alchemy and magic. As the days wore on and his investigations deepened, his encounters with the Sorcerer became brief and irregular. The Sorcerer, as he had promised, did not interfere with the course of his pupil's study, but from time to time he cautioned the younger man not to loose contact entirely with the world outside the laboratory. One evening he even suggested that a visit to the castle might be a valuable break from his studies.

"Yes, certainly," the Prince responded, his mind on other things. He was returning to the laboratory with a handful of peculiarly discolored bark. "We shall see."

"I'll be leaving soon on another collecting expedition," the Sorcerer told him. "I trust that you'll be able to take care of yourself while I'm away. I may be gone as long as a fortnight."

The Prince smiled. "Take your time. I think I'll have no trouble finding answers to any questions that might come up. Take care of yourself." He disappeared into the laboratory.

The Prince no longer had any interest in things beyond the mountaintop, had no concern for matters that were not encompassed within the four walls of the laboratory. By day he would mope about waiting for night to fall, gathering herbs and completing chores that required daylight. When Manat would finally bid him good-evening and retire to her own small dwelling, leaving him undisturbed to pursue his studies alone, then he would reverently enter the sanctuary of the laboratory and give himself wholly to the way of sorcery.

Yet at times his mind was distracted. He would find himself dawdling at the table in the flickering circle of light cast by the oil lamp, dreaming of the Sorcerer's lovely daughter, longing for her to come to him. But she would not come when prayers for her animated his trembling lips, nor when a longing ache seemed about to explode within his breast. Only after he had calmed himself with deep breathing and thoughts of emptiness, had ingested a tiny portion of the fly agaric potion which allowed him to focus his attention on his work, and had returned to his examination of the ancient texts, only when he was once again totally absorbed in the supernatural world of alchemical secrets and subtle cosmologies, only after the prayers were forgotten, the longing stilled, and she had slipped totally out of his conscious thoughts--only then would the Prince smell her scent and feel her presence within the darkened, flickering room. He learned to turn away from her to find her.

Her smile was his source of warmth on the chilly nights when a cold draft pierced the chamber from every crack and crevice. In a single glance her eyes taught him more than ten-thousand pages of text. She would discuss with him the confusing threads of thought interwoven through numerous volumes, would help him read with a comprehensive understanding pages teeming with double meanings and ambiguities, and would interpret and reinterpret for him complex passages of a book laying open before him, though she had only her memory and grasp of the subject to call upon.

"To know sorcery, you must know the world," she told him. She taught him the wisdom of the ancients. Through her he learned the curious doctrine that everything is in constant flux, ever changing and passing away, and that therefore one can never step into the same river twice. And then he learned that all is one and forever unchanging, and that the appearance of change is merely an illusion, a dream, generated by our feeble inability to grasp the whole at a single time. They laughed in wonder that the two apparently antithetical doctrines could both be true.

"Yes," the Prince responded, "they are both correct." He told her of his experience after eating mushrooms. "I have seen both truths clearly at the millstream. The single unwavering truth is comprised of an infinity of endless changes and the relentless replacement of all truths. But all the change is constantly the same."

And she taught him that we cannot experience causality directly, but can only generalize it from the perception of the consistent conjunction of events. As observers we bring to each experience the predisposition for, and the possibility of, space and time and causality through an encompassing unity of apperception, the constitutive ground for all experience.

"Yes," he told her. "I have seen that also at the millstream. I create space and time with my thoughts. Without conscious reflection, everything would be forever frozen in a series of unconnected great noontides, the eternal present, without future or past or relation between objects. Without my thoughts, things are neither above nor below, next to nor apart from, are neither separate nor conjoined. Each is merely present, and then nonexistent forevermore."

As the Prince learned from the Sorcerer's daughter, he hungered to learn more *of* her. He longed to touch her, and his desire became as palpable and sweet as syrup. He ached to enfold her in his arms and encyst her within his flesh. He was able, with the aid of the potion brewed from the fly agaric, to quell such riotous cravings. Like the moon and the earth, bound to each other, yet forever separate, she and he were destined during the days of his apprenticeship to remain at opposite ends of the oaken table. The Prince knew without having to be told that he was not yet prepared for her.

When the Sorcerer returned from his second collecting trip, the Prince asked to be allowed to finish his work in the laboratory alone and undisturbed. Seeing how adamant was the young man's resolve, the Sorcerer reluctantly agreed for the time being to let him continue his study by himself. He admonished his pupil not to ingest any of the chemicals, potions, brews, or other preparations described in the ancient writings without consulting him first. The wizard would remain available to answer any questions that might arise.

The Prince had already used up half the supply of the fly agaric. Disregarding his mentor's warning, he surreptitiously prepared yet another batch, in smaller portions this time, to make it last.

The lessons went on. She showed him how organisms develop and grow more complex through time, and how the most healthy individuals are naturally selected to survive and bear offspring to form future generations in an inherent struggle without end. She showed him the purpose of death and guided him through experiments which combined methane and hydrogen and an electric spark into the same fundamental chemical building blocks that constitute all living matter.

"Yes," he said. "I have experienced the blind unfolding of all matter and form which is neither progress nor retreat, but, rather, the mindless movement of patterns of light and darkness. Matter evolves to life, ever more complex, as a counterbalance to cosmic entropy and a coming night of dispersed radiation. Through life, the uncomprehending universe seeks to know itself for the first time."

With her gentle guidance, the Prince sampled the potions and plants and brews and unctions that produced altered states of consciousness, but he no longer slackened the dose. She knew them all and seemed able to enter his very thoughts to guide and protect him from within as he journeyed through bizarre landscapes of non-ordinary reality. He saw atoms swirling within everything and the yawning, awesome emptiness inside solid matter. He witnessed molecules interacting like errant billiard balls. He felt each tiny corpuscle of his blood seep through countless veins and arteries and capillaries to supply oxygen to a hundred billion cells. Beneath his sensitized feet the earth wobbled and spun as it whirled through the void surrounding a fading sun. He saw plants grow, watched shadows move, and perceived the universe gradually expanding. Throughout this panoply of profoundly disturbing perceptions, the single guiding star of her pure face, her gently moving grace, her tender form and body, her essence filled him, pervaded him, buoyed him up, and wafted him toward a sheltering harbor.

Late one night the Prince finished the last of the potion prepared from the fly agaric and later closed the final volume of the ancient writings. He was finished. As he pondered the future, she spoke to him of the freedom to choose.

In response, he related to her the concept of the crystal palace of rationality and the ethics of the moral imperative he had been taught at the University. Moral conduct is not free, it must conform to rational rules.

She laughed at the quaint teachings. "You are free to will the collapse of the crystal palace, for no other reason than to prove that you are free to choose, even against your own best interests. Though choice, like everything else, is an illusion, you must live as if it were the only reality. When you have mastered sorcery, you must will a world that pleases you."

"Is a sorcerer then free from the bonds of causality?" he asked her.

"A sorcerer's will and causality are one and the same." She held him transfixed with her eyes. "There is no reality to your dreams, your aspirations, your fears, your regrets. Your successes and your failures are alike an illusion. They are created by your mind, and they are as unrelated to the world presented to your senses as the sound of a single hand clapping. Sorcery is also an illusion, without substance or reality. But therein lies its power. You have seen the vast space within this solid oak table, the interactions of energy that give the appearance of substance, permanence, and power. To the man who sees beyond these illusions, truly, sorcery, though a dream, contains limitless power. Dream yourself a sorcerer of limitless power, and so you shall be. No one may oppose you unless his dream is dreamt with a greater conviction than yours." She paused. "This is your last lesson. Perhaps it is the only lesson. You will learn it well. When you have mastered the power of sorcery contained in it, you will be able to call me back."

She was gone. Right before his eyes she suddenly ceased to be. He blinked, refocused his eyes, and found that he was staring right through the place where her lovely face had been, looking at the reflection of the oil lamp in a bottle of green vegetable material on the shelf behind.

"Come back!" he cried, standing up. "We're not finished! I'm only just now beginning myself with sorcery."

Silence.

"We have much that is unfinished," he said, stretching and gazing around the room. Through the far window the sky was beginning to glow a golden orange where the sun would soon rise. "You will return to me when I have mastered sorcery," he repeated, as if by repeating it, he would seal her vow.

Still only silence.

"Then sorcery shall be mine!" He hurled the last, heavy volume the length of the room. The Prince knew with a certainty beyond certitude that she would return to him when he was ready, not as a teacher, but as a mate. "I love you," he whispered to the empty shadows, and then, marvelously exhilarated to be so near the end of his long quest, he vaulted out the door into the sobering chill of the mountain air to await the sunrise.

CHAPTER FIFTEEN

A Mystery Unveiled

The Sorcerer intercepted the Prince on the path as the young man returned from his solitary sunrise vigil. They had not spoken for a long time. Although the tattered remnants of a sublime joy still clung to him, the Prince was bone weary, and the fabric was beginning to wear thin.

"Your father has sent a messenger here to speak with you privately," the Sorcerer explained as they came around the corral fence. "Manat is getting something for him to eat. I promised him a hot bath and a warm place to sleep. He's been riding for the better part of three days." The Sorcerer directed his companion toward a small stand of cedars whose trunks glowed golden in the morning sunlight. "I told him you'd see him this afternoon. I think he intends to escort you back to the castle so the King can review your progress."

"Why must he meddle in my affairs!" The Prince's mood turned abruptly sour, and he jerked his arm free from the Sorcerer's gentle grasp. He had not slept in too many hours and was experiencing the deep irritability associated with withdrawal from the agaric elixir he had consumed for more nights in a row than he could clearly remember. "I told his other messenger that I would see him when I was ready, and not before."

"That was three messengers ago," the Sorcerer rejoined cautiously, as if he were handling a highly volatile chemical. "It's been nearly six months since you last spoke directly to one of your father's emissaries. The last two times, if you will recall, you asked me to send them away without so much as letting them set eyes on you." The Sorcerer lowered his voice. "I think you had better see this one. Your father must think something terrible has befallen you, and I'm afraid he's no longer willing to take my word alone–"

"Does the mighty Sorcerer so fear the King's wrath?" the Prince snorted. The mockery in his voice was barbed and cruel. "Where is your magic to protect you now, old man?"

The Sorcerer was alarmed by the Prince's lightning shifts of mood. He watched the younger man for a moment, then responded warily, "I have no fear for what he might do to me. My only concern is that rash action might endanger the kingdom. And you."

"I can take care of myself," the Prince swaggered. "*And* the kingdom."

The Sorcerer raised an eyebrow. He looked away toward the cottage. "I looked for you in the laboratory just now. I noticed that the drawer where I put the fly agaric was open. It was empty." He faced the Prince. "Have you been using it?"

"Yes."

"You should have consulted me first."

"Why? So you could have led me down the path of your own failures?"

"That mushroom can lead to the worst kind of madness and delusion. I don't like it. It's not safe. Without the proper guidance and discipline, it calls up great evil. If you wish to continue your studies--"

"My studies are through," the Prince snapped. "I have finished."

"Ah." The Sorcerer was obviously surprised. The morning breeze was restless with further inquiry, but the wizard restrained his curiosity. He watched the Prince quietly.

At length the Prince explained casually, "I have completed my course of study. Now I intend to undertake the actual practice of sorcery."

"Then you believe in its powers?"

"I never doubted them. You are the one who lost faith before reaching your goal, not I."

The Sorcerer turned away. Through the kitchen window of the cottage the King's messenger could be seen laboring over his breakfast. "Well then, perhaps this is the logical time for you to take a little break and go for a visit with your father. It would make him feel better, and I think you could use a–"

"I don't want to go back to the castle!" the Prince shouted. "I've got too much work to do! I've got to master this sorcery business with the utmost speed and dispatch."

"Why? What's the rush? The laboratory will wait until you return."

"But *I* cannot wait." The Prince's voice became the low growl of a crouched cat. "You know perfectly well why I can't wait, don't you?"

The Sorcerer recoiled involuntarily.

The Prince stalked him slowly. "*You* know she's been coming to the laboratory at night, don't you?"

"Who? I'm sure I don't know what you're talking about. If you've been seeing Manat, it's none of my–"

"Manat!" spat the Prince. "No, not Manat. The other one. The teacher." The Prince straightened suddenly and glanced stiffly about. Had he broken his vow by speaking of things he shouldn't to the Sorcerer? Surely the wizard knew the comings and goings of his own daughter. But why had he never mentioned her? Why all the mystery? They were using him for some purpose he could not fathom. Damn them! *I must get control of myself,* he thought. *This is a most delicate situation. I can yet win at this game by my own cunning.* He brushed the dust off the back of his robe and carefully buttoned his sleeves.

The Sorcerer watched in silence and growing alarm the outward display of a psychotic internal battle being waged before him.

The Prince's manner became direct and courteous. "I am the Crown Prince of Nod, the Heir Apparent to the throne."

"You are indeed, my lord." The Sorcerer bowed cautiously. "And you do us great honor to grace us with your presence."

"And I can do much for my friends and for my family."

"Indeed, I'm sure you can."

"I will be king, and when I am king . . . ," he paused to heighten the effect of his words, ". . . whomsoever I choose for my wife shall be the Queen of Nod."

"There is no question whatsoever about that, my lord."

The Prince smiled warmly and took the Sorcerer by the arm. "The game is over, my friend. There's no need to continue this charade any further. I concede." A twinkle was in his eye. "You've played brilliantly, and I would be the first to congratulate your victory, if only I knew the rules or object of this little game."

The Sorcerer waited quietly for a clue to what the Prince was ranting about.

The Prince released the wizard's arm, wagged a finger at him, then bowed deeply. "My esteemed friend, colleague, and teacher, I humbly ask you for your daughter's hand in marriage."

"What?"

"I know I'm supposed to wait until I've proven that I can master the ways of sorcery." The Prince smiled. "But the game is now at an end, don't you see? I shall acquire the powers of sorcery in due course. In this I swear I shall not fail you. It all comes to the same thing. The test is over. It is with the deepest humility and respect that I ask you for her hand."

"But I have no daughter," the Sorcerer protested.

"Don't toy with me any more, damn you!" snapped the Prince, the thin veneer of civility wearing through. A dull pain throbbed between his eyes and he felt mildly sick to his stomach. "I said the game is over!" He fought to regain his composure, grinned sarcastically, then bowed once more. "In case you didn't know, she has been visiting me in the laboratory late at night to teach me the ways of sorcery." He shook his fist at the magician. "I *will* have her for my wife!"

"This is very difficult, indeed." The Sorcerer settled onto the trunk of a fallen tree. "Will you be kind enough to describe for me the woman who has been visiting you in the laboratory?"

Only with great difficulty did the Prince control his temper. "If you insist, I will play along for a bit more." He bowed yet again. "She is a woman of unequaled beauty, with straight black hair that falls to her waist and pale white skin. She wears a black robe with crescent moons decorating it in white."

The Sorcerer grew pale. "Did she wear a . . . medallion?"

"Yes, of course! A silver necklace with a small silver crescent moon, as you know perfectly well."

The Sorcerer was obviously shaken. After pondering for a moment, he arose. "Come with me. I have something to show you."

He led the way around to the back of the cottage and through a small door into the storeroom. From the top of one of the high shelves near the rafters at the back, from amidst the spider webs and dust, the Sorcerer took down a large, flat crate-board box. He carried it out into the light, brushed off the dust, set it down on a flat rock, and loosened the lid. "Have you ever seen this before?"

"No. Let me see." The Prince pulled the cover away. Inside the box was a painting the Sorcerer had taken down from the wall of the kitchen years before because it brought memories too painful for him to live with day by day. Depicted was a smiling young woman holding an infant in her arms. It was the woman the Prince had just described. "Yes! That's her! Of course!" He beamed at the wizard. "She never told me her name."

"Sarai," the Sorcerer said weakly.

"Ah, yes, named after your wife."

"This *is* my wife. It's a painting of her and our daughter."

The Prince carefully lifted the painting out of the box and held it up to the sunlight. "Amazing! Your daughter has grown up to look just like her mother."

"Our daughter never grew up at all." The Sorcerer's voice was as eerie and hollow as the echo from an empty tomb. "She died more than twenty years ago, at the age of two. Of smallpox. It was she we sought to resurrect from the dead by means of these cursed black secrets of sorcery."

"No! I refuse to believe that!" The Prince shook his head adamantly. The painting dangled from his right hand. "Do you take me for a fool?"

"Perhaps you saw it at an earlier time. It used to hang on the wall of the kitchen." The Sorcerer reached carefully for the painting. "And now you have imagined–"

"No!" The Prince pushed the magician violently as he stretched forward, off balance, and the older man's heels caught against the flat rock. He tumbled over backwards and landed in the dirt with a groan. "I've imagined nothing! *The game is over.* And I'll not be trifled with anymore."

The Sorcerer sat up slowly and with a calm dignity began brushing the dust off his shoulders. "I can do nothing–"

Infuriated, the Prince threw the painting at him. "I *will* have her hand. Do you understand?" The Prince's thoughts jumped from one thing to another in random confusion. A searing pain shattered his mind into a hundred jagged shards which seemed to sparkle and flash in the blinding sunlight. He clasped his head in his hands and spun away from the seated figure. "Why are you doing this to me?" he screamed. "Damn you! The King shall have your head, and I will have your daughter, even if it must be over your dead body!"

The Prince reeled dizzily around the corner of the cottage and into the kitchen, startling Jesus, the King's messenger, as he sat stuffing himself with a second helping of Manat's cheese and broccoli omelette. Without a word of greeting he burst on through and stumbled into the sanctuary of his own tiny room, where he stood panting. He collapsed into the chair beside his writing desk. Nothing made sense. In the interior twilight his thoughts jumped between the inconsistent and the inexplicable. His eyes came to rest at last upon a small, rectangular object sitting neatly on the back corner of his desk where he had placed it the day he first arrived. As he stared at it, all the confusion seemed to drain away. He reached out and picked up the deck of cards containing nothing but threes-of-cups. He turned the cards over and over slowly in his hands, and as he did so, the conviction grew that the Sorcerer was trying to trick him even as he had tricked his father. Righteous anger welled up inside.

With the calculated calmness of an executioner, the Prince found his way back to the kitchen. Jesus had just returned to his breakfast, and when he saw the Prince enter, he stood up hastily, knocking a large chunk of goat's milk cheese onto the floor. He tried to bow and pick up the cheese in the same motion, lost his balance, stumbled into the chair, and sat down heavily on the floor. He immediately scrambled to his feet and bowed properly. "My liege," he said through a mouthful of omelette, "your father, the King, worries about you. He sends you this message:–"

"Manat!" the Prince snarled. "Leave us!"

Manat set down a pan of fried potatoes she was about to serve and left the kitchen without a word.

"Take this to the King," the Prince rasped, thrusting the deck of cards into the messenger's greasy hands. "Make haste. Tell my father the Sorcerer has tricked him. Tell him that I now command the power." He grabbed Jesus by the lapel and dragged him toward the door. "Carry my message with dispatch. Be gone with you!" He pushed the still-masticating messenger through the doorway, a napkin stuck in his collar. "Hurry!"

"But my lord, the King wants to know when he'll see you," Jesus squealed over his shoulder as he stumbled toward the stables.

"Soon," the Prince called after him. "Tell him soon."

When Jesus had disappeared over the crest, and the horse's hooves could no longer be heard, a wave of nausea washed over the Prince. He grasped the door frame and vomited into the tulips Manat had planted just outside the kitchen. Long after his stomach was empty, convulsions racked his body. When they had stopped, he crawled back inside and hoisted himself into the chair at the end of the table. His anger and frustration had flowed from him like water from behind a collapsed dam. "I have acted justly," he whispered without conviction. As a reservoir is quickly emptied when the breach is massive, the Prince was soon void of any feeling. He yawned numbly and laid his head on his arms. In a moment he was asleep.

CHAPTER SIXTEEN

The King's Great Folly

Someone had draped the Sorcerer's heavy woolen robe over the Prince's shoulders while he slept. Its rough fibers scratched his neck. Aching stiffness ran down his spine and branched into each leg when he tried to adjust his position. His bare feet were icy. The Prince opened his eyes and sat up slowly. It was late afternoon and the sun was already setting behind a small hill to the west. A chill northerly wind howled through the cedars outside and pierced the ragged cracks in the rough-hewn kitchen walls. He shivered and drew the warm cloak tighter about him, stamping his feet lightly to restore the circulation. The taste of stale bile coated his mouth.

The reality of what had transpired just before he fell asleep flooded in upon him, and the Prince gnashed his teeth. He had acted badly, had been out of control, like a spoiled brat. He tried to put the thoughts out of his mind, but he knew in his heart he must find the Sorcerer at once and try to explain. He rose unsteadily and leaned against the table. Jesus' plate had been cleared away and the dishes washed. He tottered to the door and looked outside. Someone had attempted to clean up his mess. Manat, no doubt. He filled his mouth with water from the dipper by the door, swished it around, and spat out into the yard. He filled the dipper again and drank deeply.

"Well, I've really done it this time." he said to no one. The Prince shut his eyes to hold back the tears of frustration and self-pity. The Sorcerer had been more than a teacher. He was a friend, a counselor, and an inspiration. The Prince had repaid his kindness with a cruel betrayal. It was too late to catch Jesus now, but the Prince could ride at once to the castle and assuage the fury that was almost certain to engulf the King, placate his injured ego, and perhaps subvert whatever impulse for hasty retribution the regal mind might invent. But even as he considered the reasonable course of action, the Prince knew he could not forswear his quest for mastery of sorcery just yet. He could not abandon, even temporarily, the only path that led back to the Sorcerer's daughter.

He found the Sorcerer in the laboratory, bent over a low bench gluing together the broken binding of the book the Prince had hurled across the room earlier that day. The Sorcerer looked up with an appraising eye, saw that the Prince's venom had subsided, estimated his gait to be sufficiently contrite, and turned back to his work. "Have you eaten?"

"No." The Prince hung his head. "But I'm not really hungry. I just wanted to . . . apologize for my . . . rude behavior this morning. I hope I didn't hurt you. I'm sorry."

"How could you hurt me?" the Sorcerer laughed. "Only this poor old body of mine. But I'm all right. Let's forget about it." He finished spreading the glue, pressed the loose binding firmly into place, and stacked the volume under several other heavy tomes to dry. He perched himself on the edge of the workbench. "I'm puzzled," he continued at length, "about the identity of the woman who has been teaching you sorcery."

"I'm puzzled too." The Prince sank heavily into one of the empty chairs. "In all my dealings with you, I find one consistently recurring trait, and that's constant befuddlement. That alone is predictable. I can never tell when you're telling me the truth or one of those little prevarications you're so fond of springing on my father. You admit that you've been deceiving the entire kingdom for years. For the life of me, I can't even tell whether you really believe in sorcery or not."

"All those other misrepresentations have a purpose, which I have already explained. To you alone I have disclosed the truth behind my methods. But to what end would I want to mislead you about not having a daughter?"

"I don't know." The Prince sighed. "Is it some sort of test?"

"No. I have no daughter. If I had one, I assure you I would be overjoyed and honored to give her to you in matrimony. Nothing would make me happier."

The Prince shook his head slowly. "I don't know what's going on then. I'm certain she told me she was your daughter. I didn't just make the assumption. Why would she tell me that if it weren't true?"

The Sorcerer considered the matter for a moment, then began cautiously, "Well, if you were to just assume, for the purpose of discussion, that you imagined—"

"No," the Prince interrupted quickly, though without a trace of that morning's hostility. "I can make no such assumption. She was real. She came to me too many times. I *need* this to be real. I have plans . . . ."

The Sorcerer stroked his beard for a moment, then shifted his weight. "So you intend to begin the actual practice of sorcery."

"Yes. And when I have mastered it, she will come back. You'll see. Of this I have absolutely no doubt."

"And how will you begin?"

"Precisely where you left off. Through the use of the most secret ceremonies and rites, with the aid of these potent chemicals, brews, and potions, by means of the most powerful incantations and conjurings, by giving myself utterly and without reserve to sorcery and thereby making it mine, I intend to forge a mighty protectorate that will be no mere illusion. The savages at the borders of the kingdom shall taste my fiery wrath and will shake and tremble at the mention of my name, but this time their terror will arise with good cause."

The Sorcerer had listened with increasing amusement. He bowed formally. "I shall be happy to assist you in any way I am able."

The Prince studied the older man carefully. "You don't really believe I can do it, do you?"

"I believe that you do."

The Prince, and the Sorcerer at the Prince's behest, continued collecting herbs and tubers and fungi and barks of every description from the woods and fields surrounding the homestead. They made several trips down the mountainside to obtain plants that grew only at a lower, warmer elevation. Often the Prince would send his mentor off alone to retrieve some rare or exotic element while the Prince toiled alone in the laboratory. Once again he became completely absorbed in his work and lost all track of the passing time.

A bone-chilling cold settled upon the mountaintop like a silent curse. Manat managed to keep a fire roaring in the small stove in the laboratory, and another in the kitchen fireplace. She tried to make sure that the Prince, who had grown somewhat neglectful of personal matters, was adequately dressed for the cold whenever he ventured outside.

Late one morning as the Prince was grinding dried beetle wing to powder with mortar and pestle, he was awakened from a pleasant reverie by the sound of a distant bugle. He laid down the pestle and stepped to the low window at the back of the laboratory. He pushed it open and squatted down to listen. Soon from the distance he heard again the unmistakable bugling which heralded the approach of the King's royal procession. The Prince wrapped himself in his warmest blanket and hurried outside to the crest of the hill where he would have a good view of the road winding up the mountainside.

Sure enough, about a mile below, in full dress uniform marched the soldiers who customarily accompanied the King in his infrequent peregrinations. He could not make out the individual faces, but he assumed that his father was the brightly adorned horseman in the center of the cavalcade. Already an advance guard of six bowmen was riding strong steeds over the crest of the hill not far from where he stood.

"Hoy!" he called out to them. "You're looking for me!" He hurried to intercept them on their way to the cottage. To his surprise, they ignored him, though the captain could not have missed seeing him. "Hoy!" he called again as they rushed past without slackening their speed.

Onward the horsemen thundered, and each swung a tautly strung bow gracefully off his shoulder. As they approached the cottage, bronze-tipped arrows were withdrawn simultaneously from six quivers and glistened in the sunlight.

The kitchen door sprang open. It appeared that the Sorcerer had seen the riders too. A robed specter draped in the Sorcerer's burnoose dashed from the kitchen and sprinted toward the woods.

Only then did the Prince grasp the grim intent of the six fierce bowmen.

"No!" he shouted, dashing after them. "In the name of the Crown I order you to stop! I am Crown Prince! Cease and desist at once!"

His commands were ignored. The horsemen easily rode down the fleeing figure before it reached the sanctuary of the trees. Of the six arrows which flashed across the narrowing space between hunter and hunted, three thudded into their target. The hooded figure pitched heavily forward, three feathered shafts wagging vertically above, as if in defiance of the fall.

An animal scream escaped the Prince's throat as he ran with all his might to where the soldiers were dismounting beside the fallen figure. He leapt upon the captain, screaming, "I'll have your head for this, you bastard!"

Three of the archers grabbed the Prince's arms and struggled to pull him off their leader. The captain straightened his breastplate and bowed deeply. "I am truly sorry, my liege. The King has already given me his orders, and he expressly instructed that you could not countermand them. I'm sorry." Again he bowed.

The Prince's knees grew weak as despair overtook him. The soldiers released his arms and he knelt beside the cloaked form stretched before them on the ground. There was no sign of life. The arrows had obviously pierced vital organs. Blood stained the robe and the ground. In death, thought the Prince, the Sorcerer appears smaller than ever. He grasped a shoulder and gently turned the body over.

"*Manat!*" It was not the Sorcerer at all, just his robe. Manat often wore it outside on the coldest days, as the Prince did himself at times. "My God! What have you done?"

"It was a mistake, my lord," the captain stammered. "I took her for the Sorcerer." He signaled his men to remount.

"Where are you going now?" the Prince cried.

"I'm sorry, my lord, but the King has given us orders." He swung easily into the saddle, and the horsemen started toward the cottage.

"Haven't you done enough!" the Prince called after them. He

dropped Manat's lifeless arm and raced to the house, hoping to head them off. "Stop this senseless murder!"

The soldiers were there first, and two blocked his entrance while the others searched inside. They emerged at last empty-handed. "He's nowhere to be found," the captain announced. He sent two horsemen to inform the King of developments, and over the Prince's vociferous protestations, the other four rode off, each in a different direction, to hunt the Sorcerer in the woods and fields.

The Prince turned back to the main road to confront his father, trembling with outrage, cold, and despair. He reached the summit just as the King arrived. *"What do you think you're doing?"* he screamed at his father.

"What!" the King replied. "Would you defend a man who has tried to make a fool of your father and your king?" He had expected a plea for mercy from his son, but the unbridled hostility the Prince exuded took him by surprise. Much had apparently changed since the treacherous message had been given to Jesus.

The four bowmen returned from a quick search for the Sorcerer. "We cannot find him," the captain declared.

The King raised his arms and declared a moratorium on the hunt until he had a chance to discuss matters in more detail with the Prince. This seemed to satisfy his son, so the King quickly ushered him into the privacy of the cottage, away from the soldiers, as regal propriety dictated.

Outside, the captain barked a sharp command and three foot soldiers hastily scraped out a shallow grave beneath a willow near where Manat had fallen. They wrapped her tightly in the Sorcerer's cloak, and without further ceremony, her remains were dragged to the grave and dumped in. Cold earth was thrown in on top. No one bothered to mark the grave.

At long last the King and the Prince emerged from the cottage. Things had obviously not gone well between the two. The King had never before seen his son so boldly disobedient. The lad now talked with a confidence and defiance that startled and disturbed the regent. Something of the Sorcerer's impudence seemed to have rubbed off on him. Still, the King preferred a lively argument to the apathy and melancholy that marked the last time they had talked together at the castle many months before.

"Are you sure you won't change your mind?" the King asked as he mounted his horse.

"No, father, I'll stay. I have work to do. Now more than ever."

"We will see to it that no one disturbs you." The King spoke briefly with the commander and several lieutenants. He returned to the Prince. "We will set up our camp below tonight. If you decide to come back to the castle, you may ride with us. As you know, that would please us greatly. Otherwise, we will send you our messengers regularly. Troops will be on patrol for the rest of the day."

"I don't think you'll find him, father. He's a very clever man. Please, let him be."

"We only want him brought before us. We have promised you he will not be harmed, and so it shall be. We shall see that he understands his proper place, then he will be set free." The King turned his horse haughtily. "We are now the sole sovereign power in this realm. If you need anything, let us know."

"I shall. You needn't worry about me. The kingdom itself is in grave danger, and I will do all I can to help."

The King grunted acknowledgment, smiled for an instant, and rode off at the head of the royal cavalcade.

The Prince was alone for the first time in his life, and yet he did not feel lonely. As the moon tugs at the vast oceans of the earth even when it is hidden by overcast skies, so the mere presence of the King encamped below on the mountainside awaiting his revenge pulled insistently at the gene-filled filial seas of protoplasm that constituted the Prince. His father had tried to lure him back to the castle, and unconsciously his psyche toyed with the seductive idea of returning home to warmth and peace and rest, little suspecting that it was already too late. The Prince had already ventured too far away, and home for him had evaporated utterly from the face of the cold planet.

Absently the Prince poked through the empty cottage, opening closets, peering inside crates and dresser drawers, searching beneath beds, expecting to discover what the soldiers had not, hoping the supernatural forces called up by the Sorcerer to cloud their small minds would be ineffective against one who was also privy to the mysteries of the dark science. But to no avail.

He sat down and tried to think back to when he had last seen the wizard. The Prince had been so absorbed in his own affairs that he could not be sure. Yesterday afternoon the older man had set off down the trail to gather medicinal truffles and, if possible, belly feathers from a yearling grackle, as the Prince had requested. He had not seen him return. The Prince examined the magician's neatly made bed, but he was unable to determine the last time the Sorcerer had slept in it. He knew that as long as the soldiers hovered about like angels of violence, the Sorcerer would not return.

The Prince was outraged to discover that Manat's executioners had left her hastily-dug grave unmarked. He found a large granite rock nearby and with some difficulty rolled it to her gravesite. From the workshop he retrieved a stone chisel and a wooden mallet, and because no one else had bothered, he sat down in the chill, clear mountain air to engrave a symbol of remembrance. Nothing came quickly to mind, so for want of a better idea, he spent the afternoon chiseling a crescent moon into the flat face of the rough stone.

The Prince was distressed by the Sorcerer's vanquishment before so many eyes. The King could invent stories about what had transpired, but the soldiers were bound to form opinions of their own, and those accounts would spread like a slow cancer to infect the entire organism of the state. Sooner or later tendrils of truth were bound to reach across its borders. The kingdom now lay naked and vulnerable. The Prince must prepare himself to step in and fill the enormous cavity left by the Sorcerer.

With a final careful tap he finished the stone marker, then stepped back to examine his work. Not bad for a first try. With fingers numb from the cold and arms aching, he heaved the gravestone into place as darkness fell.

For the rest of the day the King and his party sojourned in the wild brambles at the base of the mountain. There was no sign of the

Sorcerer, so the hunt was at last called off. The King bided his time uneasily. Things had not gone at all well, not at all the way he had planned. His mood grew progressively more foul, and the soldiers tried to avoid crossing his path.

In the morning the King dispatched his swiftest messenger to the Prince to see if he had changed his mind about returning with them to the castle. The rider returned before midday with a negative reply and was promptly transferred to stable duty.

"So be it!" thundered the King. He ordered the tents and provisions packed at once, and the royal party prepared for the long return journey. Before departing, the King took the precaution of assembling all his men and forced them each to swear a solemn oath never to speak of what had happened on the mountaintop the day before, upon penalty of instant death. No, things had not gone well at all.

CHAPTER SEVENTEEN

The Vindication

Once the King had departed, a black melancholy descended upon the Prince. Never had he felt so alone and helpless. For long hours he would sit in the feeble sunlight beside Manat's grave. They had never really been close, yet now that he was alone on the forsaken mountaintop, he realized that she and the Sorcerer had been like family to him, touching him more deeply than his own.

The weather grew impossibly colder. It snowed a little, just enough to enshroud the landscape with a spiritless sterility to match his mood. Without Manat and the Sorcerer to tend them, the once-roaring fires went out. The Prince managed to ignite the few sticks of dry kindling he found on the hearth to thaw his frozen fingers, but the larger logs refused to catch, and soon even the kindling was gone. He felt cold inside as well as out and took to wearing a heavy woolen blanket most of the time, which interfered with the little work he was able to begin. His mind wandered, out of his control, so that it seemed to him he was a spectator at a parade of thoughts belonging to someone else.

At night the Prince would awake from a few hours of fitful sleep cold and lonely and lost. Wrapping his blanket tightly about him, he would steal into the laboratory in search of the friendly dream that evaded him. There he would light the oil lamp hanging above the oak table, and the smell of the oil vapors and the smoke, the familiar circle of yellow light, the peculiar quiet of the low chamber, seemed to offer the only warmth he could find. In vain would he whisper to the trembling shadows just beyond the lamplight the one name that mattered, as if by uttering that terse incantation, he could call her back to the flesh and entreat her to show him what to do, where to go, who to be.   No sign of her pierced the uncomprehending darkness, however, and in the morning twilight he left the laboratory colder and more lonely than when he had first entered.

He began to experience a deep longing to return to the castle. His isolation on the mountaintop was not what he had expected it to be, and it left him weak and empty. At times he could not distinguish between the aching loneliness within him and the aching cold. Nowhere could he find the clear fire of conviction that had driven him earlier in his single-minded quest for mastery of the Sorcerer's magic. He feared the awesome responsibility which had fallen upon his untested shoulders, and he wanted to flee. Yet as surely as the moth is prisoner of the candle's searing flame, lured, entranced, and finally consumed by it, so the Prince was bound to the desolate mountaintop by his vision of the Sorcerer's daughter and his need of her.

Late one morning as he sat daydreaming beside Manat's freezing grave, trying to warm himself in the faint sunlight that filtered through a thick haze, the beating of hooves thundered into his consciousness. He turned to see the King's messenger Jesus riding over the crest of the hill and toward the cottage. Slowly, weakly, with the creaks and aches of an old man, the Prince arose and hobbled to meet him.

After bows and formal salutations Jesus produced a sealed message from his shirt and handed it to the Prince. Strange, the Prince thought, that the King would not trust an oral communication to this his most highly respected courier. "Please wait in case I wish to send a reply." He pushed his way into the privacy of the kitchen, splashed cold water on his face, and drank a dipper full. He sat down wearily at the table, and picked up the envelope. As he had been taught, he carefully examined the seal, taking more time than was really necessary, then broke it reluctantly and unfolded a short piece of paper.

"My dearest Son: Destiny undoes us cruelly. Word has passed beyond our borders that the Sorcerer has been vanquished. Please do something if you can. The King."

"So soon," he whispered, leaning back, his heart pounding violently. On unsteady knees he arose and returned to the kitchen door. "Tell the King I will do what I can. I have nothing more to tell him."

Jesus bowed once more and climbed back into the saddle. With another bow he turned and rode off the way he had come.

The Prince sat down heavily at the kitchen table, his thoughts bounding wildly across the ragged landscape of his mind. "I must pull myself together!" he commanded with an enormous exertion of will, and then lapsed again into the ubiquitous daydreams of last-second shuttleball victories and the close movement of female bodies in the musty darkness of the castle cloakroom.

As he sat immersed in fantasy, an image of the Sorcerer's daughter materialized clearly in his mind. She seemed to thrust aside the unreal with her more palpable presence, whispering to him, "I have taught you the methods. Use them!" Then the vision was gone.

The Prince shook his head to clear away the confusion. He stared at his hands folded before him on the breakfast table, opened them and felt the rough oak grain, felt the smooth fabric of his shirt sleeve. He turned to the window and the diffuse brightness hurt his eyes. He listened to the rustling of the leaves in the wind, pierced by the far-off wail of a morning dove, and he tried desperately to distinguish between what was real and what was not. To do that he would have to shut off the incessant chattering of his own thoughts. The Sorcerer's daughter had taught him the methods of meditation, and he could use her teachings to find the way.

With the fierce tenacity of the drowning man who clings to a tiny piece of flotsam, the Prince reeled into the laboratory to mix a potion from the roots of the nightshade plant to help him attain the proper state of mind. When the bitter tea had steeped, he drank it down, pulled the blanket tight about his neck, and marched out to Manat's grave to meditate. There he sat quietly, legs folded, back straight, hands cupped in his lap, his eyes fixed upon the simple crescent chipped into the marking stone. With a last, desperate exertion of will, he strove to clear his mind of every thought, every purpose, every fear and longing, everything that was or had been or ever would be, except the burning symbol of the simple crescent moon.

Hour after hour he sat thus in meditation and constant vigilance, his back and legs aching from sitting and the relentless cold, supported only by a few meager meals of goat's milk cheese and beans and frequent cups of the nightshade tea. In time a plan for the salvation of the kingdom began to formulate in the Prince's mind, and as it did, he allowed it to fill his mind and carry him along on the tide of single-minded purpose. The plan would require mastery of the deepest powers of sorcery. He would assemble all the most potent and destructive elements known to the dark magic, keep them focused under the sheer power of his will, but not combine them finally, nor utter the mightiest culminating incantations until the time was absolutely right. And when his task was accomplished, the Sorcerer's daughter would return to him.

But first, the weather, he thought. How could he be expected to produce in the laboratory and gather essential ingredients out in the woods if the hellish cold persisted? Like an athlete limbering up before the important contest, he began the preparation of an elementary concoction of beetle wings and bark which would be incorporated into a ritual to improve the climate. For three bitter, overcast days he ground, mixed, boiled, and incanted, ordering the ingredients and words through a clarity of mind his meditation and the nightshade tea made possible. In the pre-dawn darkness of the fourth day he smeared an unguent made from the nightshade roots across his forehead and neck, drank his tea, uttered the most solemn conjurations, and combined the preparation in precisely the proper sequence. He spread the mixture in a semi-circle within the ring of blackened rocks the Sorcerer used for his pyrotechnical tricks and ignited it just as the eastern horizon began to brighten. Throwing aside his heavy blanket and robes, he danced naked within the encircling flames, writhing and whirling to a prescribed step, and spoke the final secret words of darkest sorcery taught him by the ancient tombs and the Sorcerer's daughter.

The sun rose bright and warm that morning. The sky was blue and crystal clear. Birds sang and preened themselves joyfully. As the Prince slept, the snow melted away and the temperature rose steadily. In the early afternoon he awoke in a sweat and threw off the thick covers. Stepping outside into a balmy, snowless world of growing things, he felt comfortable without a shirt. The self-satisfied smile of a very powerful man languished on his lips. "I have done it."

With renewed confidence and conviction the Prince turned his energies to the implementation of his great plan. He would create a separate preparation of rare ingredients to help him attain the appropriate vision and perspective. When ingested and combined with an undisturbed mind, it would allow him to discern precisely the proper instant to unleash the awesome powers and overthrow his enemies. He began to administer an increasing regimen of chemicals, mixtures, potions, oils, rubs, snuffs, and suppositories designed to acclimatize him to the heady altitudes of the all-seeing visionary.

Late one morning the Prince was awakened by an insistent hammering on the kitchen door. He had fallen asleep at the laboratory workbench. He arose and shuffled out to find Jesus waiting at the door. "I'm sorry," the Prince said thickly, "I didn't hear you ride up. I was sleeping. Have you been here long?"

"Only a few minutes, my lord." Jesus bowed deeply. "I have an urgent message from the King or I would not have disturbed you." He produced a sealed envelope identical to the previous one. "Pleasant weather we're having. Unseasonably warm."

"Yes. Unseasonable." The Prince took the message and returned to the laboratory. He perfunctorily examined the seal and opened it.

"Dear son: As I write this, enemy forces gather to the south and east along our borders vowing our ruin. Our army will not fight, and if it does, it cannot win. We will be overrun unless you can save us. The kingdom has nowhere else to turn. Our fate is in your hands. The King."

With his heightened sensibilities the Prince had perceived for several days the growing disquiet and aggressiveness of the barbarians along the borders. Clouds of war swirled through his visions. He reread the message and returned to Jesus waiting outside the kitchen. "How long did it take you to ride with this message from the castle?"

"Two nights and the better part of two days." Jesus hung his head. "Twice I slept briefly."

"It's of no matter." The Prince shrived him with the waive of his hand. "Time is shorter than I imagined." He pondered for a moment. "Take this message to the King: Fear not, for I have mastered the powers of sorcery. I will save the kingdom."

The messenger's face brightened, and he repeated the message.

"Good. Now fly to the King with utmost haste."

Even before the horse's hoofbeats had dissolved into silence, the Prince was in the laboratory mixing together exotic ingredients for a powder, made primarily from the leaves of a semi-tropical bush, which would keep him awake and alert when he sniffed it into his nose. There would be no time to waste sleeping. The battle lines had been drawn, and he had to be ready when the enemy broke over the kingdom like storm surf upon the low strand.

The following days were a blur of non-stop activity for the Prince as he prepared to join battle with the barbarian hordes. From time to time he quaffed down a potion of nightshade tea and sat on the crest of the hill not far from Manat's grave to watch the distant movements of all but invisible enemy forces. With his heightened perceptions he seemed to be able to hear commands barked down the ranks, from commander to captain to lieutenant to sergeant to squad leader to soldier as the invaders made ready. He could feel the cold steel of the battle swords that were oiled and honed and polished by the thick fingers of fifty-thousand savage warriors, could feel the intensity of bloody hate which was about to explode from the south and east, and the vision chilled him. He regretted having no fly agaric left to use in his conjurings and no way to obtain more. It could prove essential in reaching the proper concentration to focus the awesome powers he would soon be calling up.

Again and again the Prince snorted the white powder to clear his head and fight off sleep. As he conjured and wrought the magic that would rain down upon the barbarians, he would augment his perspective and bolster his energies with a taste of mushroom here and a sip of tuber tea there. He sought to achieve the benign distance of a surgeon. He lost all track of the days and nights and tuned his entire being to the task of preparation for the final conflict. At precisely the instant the barbarians sullied the sacred soil of the realm with ten-thousand pairs of feet, the battle would be waged and won. At that precise instant his conjuring and his alchemy would come together into an enormous fireball which he would direct from the mountaintop with the sheer energy of his will to incinerate the invading devils.

The endless preparations finally drew to a close. Two great oaken vats held complementary portions of the mighty elixir which would soon be spilled together to form the chemical basis for his power. The preliminary incantations were recited in the prescribed order, and only the final terse epithets required uttering to bring into play the spiritual counterpart of the supernatural forces. The Prince had brought the undertaking to the brink of completion with an unhurried solemnity and careful attention to detail that the Sorcerer's daughter had taught him so well, and yet his heart was troubled and his confidence was shaken. An important ingredient seemed to be missing.

From his lofty perspective, the Prince saw that the enemy to the south had already begun to board the rough boats in a massive flotilla which would soon carry them across the Great River to assail the kingdom. To the east, in a high mountain valley, rabid hordes swilled a foul liquor and danced themselves into a frenzy to be unleashed upon the realm in coordination with the attack of the southern host. The Prince hung his head. There was little time to spare, and he was not prepared.

He wandered listlessly along the crest of the mountain and found himself at Manat's grave, which he had ignored lately. He sat quietly and began to collect his mental powers. Something was missing. He gazed at the crescent moon on the tombstone.

A glint of bright red caught his eye from the shadows of the willows just behind the stone. The Prince stood up to investigate. A shaft of sunlight lanced the darkness of the trees and illuminated an object on the ground. He approached warily. Emerging like a periscope from the rich soil beneath the willows rose the fruiting body of a large mushroom. The Prince bent over in amazement. Before him was the unmistakable red-and-white-speckled cap of fly agaric protruding obscenely from the earth. He wept in astonishment at the incredibly propitious sign. Tenderly he plucked the bright mushroom and bit off the cap, chewed the pulpy fungus slowly as if partaking of an essential sacrament, with his entire being tasting the familiar flavor, and with great reverence swallowed it down. Success was assured. He no longer harbored any doubts.

The time had come for the Prince to prepare himself. He washed in accordance with the ancient rites and put on the Sorcerer's fire-red ceremonial robe with the crescent moon emblazoned on the back. He prepared a powerful liquor and drank it down in a single draught. To the bung plug of each of the vats he carefully tied a rope and ran a line out to the crest of the hill, to a place not far from Manat's grave, a little hillock he had solemnized in a brief ceremony earlier that day. There he sat, summoning up his energies in a last contemplative moment before the holocaust.

As he rested thus, certain that completion was at hand, yet unsure of the ultimate outcome, the wispy haze before him high above the valley floor seemed to take on the shape of two figures. He watched in awe as the two forms grew brighter and more distinct, and the Sorcerer and his daughter, arm in arm, floated before him in midair.

"My friends!" he cried, scrambling to his feet. "I knew you would not forsake me."

"We cannot help you," the Sorcerer cautioned, his voice as empty and haunting as the wind. "This test is yours alone, and it cannot be otherwise."

"But will I succeed? Can I defeat these terrible armies with sorcery?"

"Have no doubt about it," the Sorcerer's daughter whispered, her words almost indistinguishable from the wind. She held the Sorcerer's arm and smiled serenely.

"Thou mayest defeat thine enemies," the Sorcerer proclaimed, piercing him with his bright eyes, "by madness."

"My madness, or theirs?" the Prince asked.

"Is there a difference?" replied the Sorcerer. Then he and his daughter floated up and away and vanished like the mist dispersed by the wind.

"Come back!" cried the Prince, but he knew that they would

not. The trial was to be his alone. Had the Sorcerer not said as much? The time for action was at hand.

He turned to face the enemy, legs spread for balance and feet firmly planted. Hundreds of miles to the south and the east the Prince perceived the hostile armies inching toward grim destinies. He allowed himself to think for a moment longer of the Sorcerer's daughter. She shall be mine, he vowed, when this task is finished. He felt as if he were floating several inches above the ground. From the ceremonial robe he took a special dangerous mixture of ground devil's root, powdered mushroom, and dried leaves from the nightshade plant, and poured it into the bowl of a tiny pipe he held in his left hand. He lit the mixture and drew down the acrid, pungent smoke as barbarians ships reached the shore.

His right hand pulled taut the rope that ran to the vats, and he uttered the culminating caustic incantation. Then he waited for what seemed an eternity of blissful completion.

The boats beached, and savage warriors scrabbled ashore. At the same instant the Prince yanked hard on the rope and jerked the bung plugs out of both vats. The steaming mixtures rushed together foaming and bubbling and hissing as they formed an enormous, turbulent pond in the natural bowl of the mountaintop. Suddenly the mixture exploded into a massive fireball which engulfed the cottage, roiling and churning, but seemed neither to rise nor to burn itself out.

"*Zap!*" the Prince spat, bringing the first finger of his right hand down in a throwing motion, pointing south at the center of the advancing troops. A large gob of the burning ball tore free from the mass and shot down the line he pointed. Miles away the fireball struck the enemy warriors, engulfing them, blistering screaming lungs and throats, burning them. The Prince perceived it all with a savage vividness. He witnessed each single hair burn, each piece of flesh blacken and curl, each charred bit of clothing unravel, each glowing sword fall hissing back into the swirling waters of the Great River.

"*Zap!*" he screamed again, launching a fireball to the right, and "*Zap!*" another to the left of the smoking gap in the enemy ranks. "*Zap! Zap! Zap!*" Again and again the Prince blasted the southern army with his inconceivably deadly weapon, bowling over and engulfing the straggling hordes who were now in headlong, wild retreat back across the turbulent waters.

When none of the southern invaders was left alive, the Prince turned his attention to the army trembling in the mountain pass to the east. The soldiers bolted in confusion and disarray after witnessing the unbelievable spectacle of power unleashed against their southern allies. But the Prince showed no mercy. One by one he directed fireballs into the ragged mountain enclaves, hunted down every hostile soldier, and incinerated them one and all.

As the raging fires of total destruction burned out, dying away to smoke and embers, the Prince thought he could hear the joyous cheers of the King's army below. The soldiers in the front lines threw down their weapons and turned as one person to the Sorcerer's mountain in awe and respect. It seemed to the Prince as he stood there on the brink that, as the news spread, the citizens of each village and town and city poured out into the streets to pay him solemn homage. He raised his arms in recognition, though he knew they could not see him from so far away.

"The kingdom has been saved!" they seemed to shout. "Long live the Prince, our new Sorcerer and Protector!"

The enemies of the realm vanquished and his course of action vindicated by the burned-out armies, the Prince found his peace at last. Although engorged with the powders, potions, herbs, and draughts that had borne him to victory, he nonetheless ate the stem of the fly agaric he had placed in his pocket and choked down the last of a foul-tasting brown leaf to give him the strength to finally call the Sorcerer's daughter back. By sheer force of will he fought off an overwhelming exhaustion. For a moment he seemed to be fighting through reality as thick as earth and mud.

The Sorcerer's daughter was there beside him. Though his hands ached and his fingernails were clotted, he reached out and grasped her hand. It was the first time they had ever touched, and the gentle pressure of her slim fingers sent mighty volts of electricity through his staggered body and reeling brain.

They sat together on the rim of the Sorcerer's mountain and watched the sun set before them. It sank into a dark land of exquisite beauty he had never noticed before. There were no enemies in that direction, no questions nor confusion, no uncertainty, no old age, sickness, nor death. His heart was suddenly filled with the longing to go there, to the fine land into which the sun was sinking, just the two of them to dwell forevermore in happiness. And the power of alchemy did not fail him. He could feel the fretful wound that separated self from other beginning to close. Together, without speaking a word, hand in hand, they reached blissfully outward and flew off over the Kingdom of Nod to that land of forgotten joy and peace, guided by the vision of a frog wielding a flaming sword which turned every way.

EPILOGUE

An Alternative Reality

The invading armies overran the inept, ragtag defenders of the Kingdom of Nod in the first day. The onslaught of barbarians, unchecked as it was by any military resistance, was slowed only by the time it took the raiders to pillage, rape, lay waste, and sate themselves totally on the blood and flesh of the once orderly kingdom.

The King awaited his fate in the castle. His counselors and retainers had abandoned him to flee before the onrushing hordes. He was alone and frightened in the brittle sanctuary of his throne room, and for an instant he contemplated self-destruction to spare himself humiliation at the hands of the invaders. "Surely the Prince will save us at the last minute," he muttered over and over to himself, as if by saying it, it would miraculously be so. His decision not to take his own life was the last great mistake of his reign. The barbarians dragged him before the jeering troops. They witnessed his horrible, screaming death as the commander himself slowly tore the skin off his royal body. He gave up his life without a trace of dignity.

As soon as all resistance was suppressed, the warriors from the south and east turned upon one another to fight over the spoils of the kingdom. In time the eastern army advanced as far as the road that led up the side of the Sorcerer's mountain. A small contingent rose along the trail toward the summit. Near the crest, where the road passed directly below the edge of the fire-blackened plateau which had once been the homestead of the Sorcerer and his wife, they came upon the dead Prince. His body was badly bloated, and in his twisted right hand he held the hand of the dead and decomposing servant girl Manat whose rotting corpse he had exhumed with his naked hands from the shallow grave nearby.

The soldiers refused to pass that spot. The Prince's lifeless, grinning visage held permanently frozen a mask of conquest, a contemptuous sneer of mastery over all the merely worldly elements. They took him for the Sorcerer himself and were frightened beyond reason. The unholy specter sapped whatever rapacity remained in the conquerors and left them uneasy.

Over the crest of the hill a forward patrol descended from the direction of the burned-out cottage and joined the main force where it was stalled below the grisly vision. With them was an aged gentleman in ragged robes they had found poking through the rubble of the old homestead. His hair was silver-gray and his eyes burned with an eerie fire. His wrists were bound with rawhide.

"Do you know him?" the Captain demanded of his prisoner, pointing to the corpse of the Prince.

"I knew him."

"So this was your powerful Sorcerer."

The old man shrugged. He held out his bound wrists.

"Did he really possess the awesome powers to thwart our invasions, or did we just imagine them?" the Captain asked, as if the old man might somehow know.

He shrugged again. "Is there a difference?"

The Captain pulled a knife from his belt. "What happened to him?" He cut the cords that bound the prisoner.

"It appears to me that his last lesson was a bit too much for him," the old man replied, rubbing his wrists. "May I go?"

The Captain looked him over. He had no property and was obviously no threat to the invasion. The war was over. It was the Captain's turn to shrug. He watched the old man limp his way down the rough trail, passing through the nervous troops like a ghost, and disappear around the hillside below.

The Captain looked out across the vanquished kingdom and sighed. He sniffed the breeze. Rain clouds were gathering to the west.

www.ingramcontent.com/pod-product-compliance
Lightning Source LLC
Chambersburg PA
CBHW060827120626
46557CB00001B/400